BACK-ALLEY BRAWL

Turning the corner into the dark alley, Fargo put his hand on the butt of his pistol. As he did, he saw movement from the corner of his eye. A young boy rushed from the shadows. Fargo went into a crouch and started to draw, but stopped. He wasn't going to shoot a child. Then he heard the heavier tread of a large man behind him. The boy had been a diversion.

Fargo dodged, twisting around as the heavyset man swung a club that grazed the side of Fargo's head. Stars exploded along with pain. Staggered, he pulled his six-gun.

"Hold it," he said. "I don't want to shoot, but I will."

He heard the whistling of a club the instant it crashed into the back of his head, and dropped to his knees. His last thought before falling was that the boy he thought was nothing more than a diversion had just taken him out.

"Don't worry," Amanda said quietly. "I will order. What do you want?"

"I could eat an entire cow," Fargo said. "Raw."

"Tartare?" Then Amanda laughed. "Trust me. I will make certain you get a decent meal."

"How are we going to pay for it?" asked Fargo. "I don't have much money left."

"Oh, that might be a problem. I certainly did not bring money," she said, as if that was something unclean. "I always let Randolph handle such things."

Fargo didn't have to point out that her manager was dead and, by now, buried in an Oakland cemetery because the thought obviously occurred to Amanda. A tear formed in the corner of her eye. She dabbed at it with the corner of her linen napkin.

"Mr. McGuire will pay dearly for inconveniencing me the way he has. He shall start paying this very moment. Yes!" she said, coming to a conclusion that Fargo did not understand. "Eat what you will. I shall see to it that Horatio McGuire pays for it all!"

Fargo was bewildered by an army of waiters, each bringing different items to the table. He watched Amanda like a hawk, duplicated what she did, and hoped he did not make too much of a fool of himself. Seeing his uneasiness, Amanda leaned forward and whispered to him.

"You will never be out of place at any gathering if you eat slowly, smile cheerfully, and nod often."

Fargo had to laugh. "That sounds like good advice whether you're in a high-class place like this, or facing down a grizzly."

"There's not much difference," Amanda allowed. After that, the meal went quickly. Fargo was even enjoying himself when the maître d' came over, the check on a silver salver. He started to push it toward Fargo when Amanda reached out and tapped him on the wrist with her fan.

"Do be a good soul and put that on Mr. McGuire's bill."

The maître d' paused.

"You *do* know Mr. Horatio McGuire, don't you? He owns the Montgomery Street Melodeon, a venue of quite good repute." She batted her eyelashes in the man's direction and fixed him with her dancing gray eyes.

"You know Mr. McGuire?"

"He brought me here from . . . Europe," Amanda said, changing the location to make the maître d' more amenable to her persuasive wiles.

"But of course I shall do so, mademoiselle."

"Very good," Amanda said, patting her lips with her napkin. "Now be a good man and get us a carriage to take us directly to the theater. I would not want to be late on this night."

"But no," the maître d' said, totally under Amanda's spell now. "I will call up the finest carriage in all of San Francisco!"

"Do you think McGuire will pay for our meal?" Fargo asked as he escorted Amanda from the restaurant. It galled him to foist a bill off on a man he had never met, even if he could never have paid for this in a month of Sundays.

"He owes me," Amanda said simply. "Help me into the carriage."

Fargo looked up in surprise to see the same cabdriver who had driven him to the Regent Hotel. The driver's eyes widened when he recognized Fargo.

"Good to see you again, sir," he said, his manner totally different now.

"To the Montgomery Street Melodeon," Fargo said. He leaned back in the seat, Amanda pressed close to him. The foggy night closed in around them and let him believe they were drifting alone, only faint sounds in the rest of the city intruding on his dream.

Before he knew it, the cab rocked to a halt.

"Here we are," the cabdriver said.

"Mr. McGuire will pay you," Amanda said as Fargo helped her down. The driver started to say something, then clamped his mouth shut.

"I'll see you get paid," Fargo told him.

"Sir, would it be all right if I waited for you? You'll need a carriage after the performance, and I'd be honored."

Fargo marvelled at the change in the man's demeanor. He nodded, held out his arm and escorted Amanda up the broad steps in front of the theater. Fargo looked around as they walked and decided the Montgomery Street Melodeon was everything Amanda had said and more. The steps were white marble, and the huge pillars marching along the front like stone soldiers might have been as well. The broad double doors opened into a vast lobby appointed in red velvet and gilt edges.

Fargo found himself staring at large posters glued to the walls. One in particular drew him. He stared for a moment and then turned to Amanda, "That's you. Amanda Fredericks."

"So it is," the blonde said, wrinkling her nose in distaste. "What a terrible likeness."

The drawing looked a great deal like Amanda, but since she did not like it Fargo said nothing more. However, his eyes kept drifting back to the poster advertising the new play starring Amanda.

"McGuire is around somewhere," she said irritably. "I know it. I can *feel* him. The sockdolager is here."

"Is that him?" Fargo asked. A man of immense girth came downstairs from an office to the left of the lobby. The diamond stickpin in the man's cravat shone like a small star in the nighttime sky, and the rest of his clothing matched the richness of his jewelry.

"You!" cried Amanda. "Horatio McGuire!"

"Might I be of assistance?" the man asked, huffing and puffing from the exertion of walking downstairs. "For such a lovely lady, your wish is my command."

"I demand a command performance!" cried Amanda.

McGuire looked at her, then frowned. "I have a fine actress under contract already. Perhaps we can find some part for you. If you can sing, perhaps a choral part?"

"You have *me* under contract, you fool!" raged Amanda. "My manager was killed by brigands. I've been shot at and almost robbed. Why, the trip has been exasperating and deadly!"

"Amanda? Amanda Fredericks?"

"Who else might you have under contract?" Amanda glowered at him.

"You weren't supposed to arrive until next week. This is most irregular. How did you happen to come so early?"

"Early? My contract is explicit. Tonight is the night I open!"

"There is some mistake. See the placard! It specifically

says you open *next* week. Let's examine the contract. You say your manager is dead?" McGuire stared at Fargo, silently wondering who he might be and why he escorted Amanda.

"I have no idea what poor, dead Randolph did with the contract. He handled my business dealings."

"Is this your new manager?" McGuire asked, still puzzling out Fargo's role.

"No, not at all. Mr. Fargo is . . . a friend. He rescued me from the robbers."

"I see," McGuire said, dismissing Fargo entirely now. "Come, my dear Miss Fredericks. My office is a more comfortable venue for discussing such matters. I have a bottle of fine brandy, should you be interested in a drop or two to cut the trail dust on your canary-like vocal chords."

"You are too kind," Amanda said as she took McGuire's pudgy arm and let him steer her toward the flight of stairs he had just descended. She bent close and chattered like a magpie as they began the long trudge up the steps. McGuire hung on her every word, even laughing in delight once or twice until they reached the top of the stairs and vanished down a corridor.

Fargo let Amanda go since she seemed to be in her element now. Having settled the matter of why McGuire had not sent a brass band to greet her allowed Amanda to concentrate on other matters. Fargo backed off, then turned and left the theater since he still had a package to deliver.

He might have failed to give Clay Nance his inheritance before, but he would not make the same mistake twice. Fargo hurried back to the Regent Hotel, changed into his dirty, tattered buckskins, and again set out for Sydney-Town to find Nance.

5

Fargo had been stalked before and knew the feeling. He felt that now. The only difference was that now he was walking the foggy streets of San Francisco and not a game trail in a deep forest. He skirted the bagnio where Bangers still called out raucously for passersby to sample the illicit offerings inside. More than one sailor went into the deadfall. The fog that had obscured the streets during Fargo's earlier foray into Sydney-Town now floated about in wispy veils, dragging damp fingers across his face and sometimes giving him a view of the entire street ahead before closing in again to blindfold him.

Fargo kept close to the buildings, preferring to have something solid along his right side in case he was attacked. After a few minutes of prowling about like a hunted animal, his better sense asserted itself. There was nothing to be afraid of. He had survived this long because of his abilities, and would get out of this perilous section of town populated by cutthroats and riffraff exiled from Australia.

Walking more boldly, Fargo felt better, and his confidence returned. When he had come into Sydney-Town before, he had not realized he had to be wary of everyone he met, including small children. He knew now and was alert but not anxious. He stretched and the bruises and aching muscles that tattooed his body reminded him of his carelessness.

He held up the scrap of paper with the instructions for finding Larson's Lair, looked around, got his bearings and kept moving down the street, away from the side street where Bangers had sent him before. Three blocks farther he found a brightly lit, rowdy tavern with a fistfight going on just inside the door. It quickly spilled out into the street. Fargo stepped back and watched the two huge men pummel each other with blows powerful enough to fell a redwood. The potent punches landed, but neither man seemed to take much note.

A short, solidly built man came from inside the saloon, swinging a stubby wooden club. He stepped into the fray, whaling away at both men. One blow landed on the side of the larger man's head, knocking him to the ground.

"It's about time, mate!" cried the other fighter, stepping back. "I was beginnin' to think you'd never come to me aid!"

The man with the club turned, swinging in a wide arc that ended on the larger man's forehead. The thud of wood smashing into bone echoed down the street, followed quickly by the sound of the man hitting the street. A quick gesture with the club brought two more rowdies boiling out of the saloon. The three set about robbing the two fighters.

Fargo slipped into the saloon and looked around the smoky interior. He didn't know Clay Nance by sight, but figured he would look like his brother.

"Whatcha want, mate?" asked the man with the club as he pressed back into the saloon. He poked Fargo with the end of his weighted cudgel to pin him against the wall.

"I'm looking for someone," Fargo said, not wanting to share his business with such an openly petty thief.

"You ain't welcome," the man said. "This here place's only for the Sydney Ducks."

"Ducks?"

"This is Sydney-Town and us Sydney Ducks run it the way we like. Now blow on outta here."

Fargo wasn't budging. Arthur Nance had thought his brother frequented this place, although Clay Nance was hardly Australian. If Clay Nance was not here, someone who was might provide directions to finding him.

"That's mighty annoying the way you're poking me with your stick," Fargo said.

"Well, now, ain't that ducky?"

Fargo was ready for the man's next move. He reared back to ram the end into Fargo's belly. When the club moved, so did Fargo. The blunt end slid past and crashed through the flimsy saloon wall, momentarily pinning it. Fargo moved fast. He grabbed the man's wrist, spun, and smashed his elbow into the side of the man's head, sending him to the floor.

When the dazed man stirred, Fargo twisted hard on the wrist he still held.

"Try that again and I'll break off your hand and beat you to death with it."

"You—" sputtered the man. "Lemme go!"

Fargo released his grip. The man clutched his hand, holding it close to his body.

"You busted me hand, ya did."

Fargo ignored the complaint. He looked around the saloon, hoping to see Nance. Three men fought each other in the rear, not caring who they hit as they stumbled and struggled around. Two tables covered in green felt were occupied by serious gamblers. Others—all Sydney Ducks, Fargo guessed from the curious way they dressed—bellied up to the bar, drinking one shot of rotgut after another.

"You'll pay, you will!"

Fargo half-turned and kicked hard. The toe of his boot crashed into the man's chest, knocking him back against the wall.

"You're starting to annoy me. A word of advice. Don't annoy me."

"Nobody gets into Larson's Lair who's not a Duck!"

"Then how did Clay Nance get in?" asked Fargo, watching the bouncer's reaction carefully. The man's beady eyes darted to the card game in the far corner of the room before coming back to stare up into Fargo's cold blue eyes.

"He's one of us. He's a Duck! He spent time in the diamond fields outside Chapman Gulch at Echunga with me!"

"If you're a friend of his, then you won't mind me talking to him about his family."

"You—" The bouncer tried to get back to his feet. Fargo yanked the club out of the wall and brought it down on the top of the man's head. This time the bouncer lost all interest in trying to block Fargo from entering the saloon.

Fargo looked around to see if anyone minded the way the saloon bouncer had been treated. If anyone noticed, they made no move to stop him. He went to the table where four men played cards. Fargo knew serious playing when he saw it—and this was a serious game. Close to a thousand dollars rested in the pot.

"Nance?" Fargo said loudly. He looked over the four and couldn't pick out Arthur's brother until one of them glanced up.

"Why'd Charlie let you in? You're not a Sydney Duck."

"Your brother never mentioned that you were," Fargo said.

"Arthur? You know Arthur? Well, why didn't you say so?" Clay Nance turned and kicked the chair out from under the man next to him. "Have a seat," he invited, pointing to the chair recently and precipitously vacated. "How's the old bastard?"

"You don't look a thing like him," Fargo said, not sure he wanted to give this man the package he carried until he was certain of his identity.

"Arthur's me younger half-brother," Nance said. "Same mother, different fathers. Mine was a sailor."

"Australian," guessed Fargo. He saw he was right.

"He was lost at sea. Mum remarried. A boring bloke. An accountant he was, but he did the right thing by adopting me. Arthur came along a while later."

Fargo knew Clay was older and being half-brothers explained the difference in their physiques. He still wasn't certain this man was Clay Nance, not in a den of thieves and liars.

"Arthur's dead," Fargo said. If he had doubted this was Clay Nance, the expression on the man's face erased any question.

"What happened? I haven't been in touch with him for a while, but he was fit as a fiddle the last I heard."

"Cancer," Fargo said simply. "It came on fast."

"Sorry to hear that. I promised Mum I'd look after him. Feel like I let 'em both down."

"He wanted you to have this. It was his only request."

"You and him was tight, eh?"

"He was a friend," Fargo said. He handed over the package.

Clay Nance ripped off the oilcloth wrapper and tore open a cardboard box to reveal a small lacquered box.

"Fancy that. My pa bought this from Shanghai and gave it to our mum."

Fargo stood and started to leave.

"Wait!" Clay Nance said, looking up at him. "I owe you for bringing me this when I needed it most."

"How's that?" asked Fargo, wondering what Nance meant.

"I would've had to fold if I hadn't got some money." Clay Nance opened the box and worked his fingernail under a false bottom to pry it open. Inside lay a small padded leather bag. Fargo sucked in his breath as Nance opened the pouch and spilled out a half dozen glittering diamonds.

"I'll see your hundred and buck up another hundred," Nance said, facing the man across the table from him.

He shoved the box in Fargo's direction. "Here you go, lad. For your trouble."

"You don't want the box?"

"Only what was in it. Good old Arthur. He had a way of bailing me out when I needed it most." Clay Nance turned back to his game with the other Sydney Ducks, ignoring Fargo now that the betting had started to get fast and furious.

Fargo hoped Nance won his hand. Otherwise, giving him his brother's diamonds would have been for naught.

As he walked out, Charlie struggled to get to his feet. His right hand hung limp and broken, but in his left he held a wicked thin-bladed flensing knife.

"You ain't gonna—"

This was as far as he got before Fargo stepped closer, knocked the knife away, and drove his fist squarely into the point of the man's chin. Charlie's head snapped back and he sank to the floor, knocked out cold by Fargo's single punch.

No one in Larson's Lair took notice, not even Clay Nance.

Fargo considered changing back into the fancy clothes he had left at the hotel, then decided against it. He was comfortable in his buckskins, dirty and tattered as they were. His long stride crossed San Francisco, leaving Sydney-Town far behind with all its vices and open lawlessness. The entire time Fargo had been in this end of town, he had not spotted a single lawman. Considering how dangerous the place was, they would need to travel in packs.

Fargo knew he ought to have felt relief at being free of the obligation to Arthur Nance, but he wasn't. He had expected more gratitude from Clay Nance. Fargo held up the lacquered box he had carried halfway across the country to give to Nance. It had been foolish of him to think Nance would appreciate it any more than he had. Fargo started to toss the box into the gutter, but stopped. The bright lacquer caught distant gaslights and reflected like an iridescent-green June beetle. The intricate patterns fascinated Fargo as he traced out a writhing dragon, a tiger, and several animals he could not identify.

He wrapped it up again and decided to keep it to remind him to be more careful when he made promises, even to a dying man. Still, Fargo's agreeing to deliver the box had eased Arthur Nance's mind and let him die a little happier. Fargo doubted Arthur had any idea his brother—half-brother—would care for nothing but the diamonds in the false bottom.

The San Francisco streets were quiet under their veil of fog until he reached the Montgomery Street Melodeon. Carriages dropped off patrons and well-dressed men and women hurried up the broad steps for the final show. Fargo walked around the block and saw a large, elaborately artistic poster glued to a wall advertising one final week of the dramatic play, *Richelieu*, starring Desirée Lefanu. Fargo looked at the dates and figured that this would run until Amanda's play started the following week.

He went to the stage entrance and wondered if he could get inside to see Amanda one more time. Fargo remembered fondly the bath they had taken together and wanted to part on equally pleasurable terms, but now that the had delivered Clay Nance's inheritance, his inclination to stay in San Francisco for a few days had evaporated.

Only Amanda could convince him to change his mind, and he saw that he might not be allowed to see her. After all, he was roughly dressed and not likely to be allowed into a theater where so many richly appointed people gathered.

He knocked on the stage door and heard someone scurrying around inside. He stepped back in time to keep from having the door bang him in the face. A dark-haired, wild-eyed young woman stood with her hand on the knob, looking as if she would rush into the night at any moment.

"How dare he!" she cried. "I am the star. He has no right to do this to me, to Desirée Lefanu!" She turned hot, angry eyes on Fargo, as if trying to melt him so she could get past.

"You're the star of *Richelieu*," he said, remembering her name from the poster.

"Ha! You see! Even the lowest of the scum from the gutters recognizes me! I am the star and yet he—he—oh!" She sputtered as she whirled about and stalked back into the theater.

Fargo caught the door and followed. An elderly man sat in a chair beside the door. Fargo almost laughed as he thought of this frail old man and compared him to the bouncer at Larson's Lair in Sydney-Town. Then the laughter died on his lips when he saw the old man had two six-shooters shoved into his belt and hidden under his coat. From the worn grips, both six-guns looked well used.

"Who the hell are you?" the old man demanded.

"I'm a friend of—"

"If you say Desirée, you'll get tossed out," the man warned, turning a watery eye on Fargo.

"I'm a friend of Amanda Fredericks," he said.

For a moment, the old man stared, then burst out laughing. "Now don't that beat all? Are you really?"

Fargo nodded.

"Come on in, but you got to be quiet. Not like that bitch." The man pointed down a narrow corridor running away from the wings where Desirée argued with someone just out of Fargo's line of sight.

"What caused the commotion?" Fargo asked, kneeling beside the man's chair. He wasn't sure which creaked more as the old man sat, the chair or the man's knees.

"If you're a friend of Miss Fredericks, you ought to know. She took over the starring role for the final week."

"In *Richelieu*?"

"She won't start *East Lynne* until next week. Mr. McGuire figured she might as well finish Desirée's run."

"And Miss Lefanu didn't take kindly to it," Fargo finished.

"Desirée wasn't pulling the crowds like she did before. Truth is, she's a terrible actress. All she can do is show a bit of leg. She might as well go to the Bella Union or the Opera House if she wants to do that kind of play. Leg shows. Pah!"

"From what I saw, she has a really pretty leg to show," Fargo said.

"Not as pretty as Miss Fredericks," the old man said, grinning.

Fargo wasn't going to argue that. He had seen Amanda's legs all the way up and liked every inch.

"Amanda's onstage now?" Fargo tipped his head to one side and listened to the applause from the theater. He thought he heard her voice over the applause, but could not be sure.

"They've got another half hour to go. Would you believe it? Desirée's been running around, throwing a tantrum for most of an hour, ever since the play started and she wasn't out there in the footlights. This might be her best acting yet."

"My name's Fargo," he said by way of introduction.

The old man thrust out his hand. "Reggie Hall. I used to own the Market Melodeon but it went belly up and took me with it. So I retired. Can't get show business out of my blood, though. That's why I pick up a few dollars—damned few!— and hang around backstage. No matter what the show or who's starring, they all act the same."

"Like spoiled children?" asked Fargo, watching as Desirée continued her tirade.

Reggie laughed and nodded. "There's Miss Fredericks now, coming off to take a breather."

Fargo went to the wings and looked out to where two costumed actors pretended to fight each other with wooden swords.

"Skye, you're back. How wonderful that you came to see me. Horatio decided to let me open tonight. Not in the play we had agreed upon, but Randolph *is* dead and could not complain. This is such a wonderful story."

"You already know the lines?"

"Of course I do. I'm an actress." Amanda frowned. "I'm afraid we are a few extras short tonight."

"Did some of them walk off to protest Desirée losing her starring role?" he asked. Amanda looked at him as if he intentionally had shoved his head into a bear's mouth.

"Whatever are you saying? No one quits a job because an actress is replaced. It's too hard finding new roles, even in a town as rife with theaters as San Francisco. Who knows why the extras didn't show up. Drunk, perhaps."

"If they're extra, you don't need them, do you?"

"Oh, Skye, you don't know *anything* about the theater. They're not superfluous, they're background, as important as the scenery." She stepped back and looked him over. Amanda pursed her lips and then said, "You will do just fine."

"What are you talking about?"

"You can be an extra." She motioned to a harried man clutching a fistful of papers. "You there, the one who is directing. I forget your name. Use Mr. Fargo as an extra."

The director eyed him skeptically and shook his head.

"He doesn't look much like an Indian, but the buckskins are a nice touch. All right," the director said, coming to a quick decision. "You're on in one minute."

"What do I do?" asked Fargo, startled at how fast everything was moving around him. He would rather have gone back to the Sydney Ducks' saloon and taken them all on in a big free-for-all than stand in front of a theater filled with rich, well-dressed men and women.

"Don't worry, Skye, you're a natural." Amanda straightened her skirt and lifted her bosoms, let them bounce about a moment, then rushed out. Fargo watched and then felt the director's hands on his shoulders, shoving him onstage in front of five hundred theatergoers.

6

The next thing Fargo knew, Amanda was pushing him back onto the stage to take a bow. He watched what the others did and followed suit. Staring at the audience struck him numb. He had faced stampedes and Indians wanting to lift his scalp, road agents and mountain lions, and had never been so paralyzed. It wasn't fear. He couldn't say what it was. Worst of all, he liked it.

"You were a natural, Skye!" enthused Amanda, who stood on tiptoe, pressed her half-exposed breasts against his chest and kissed him. She bounced away like a child's ball, shaking hands and kissing the others onstage. The curtain had fallen, cutting off the audience, but Fargo heard their thunderous applause.

"What did I do?" he asked to no one in particular.

"You stood there like a tree in the forest," Reggie Hall said, shuffling onstage. "That's all you had to do. You were an Indian brought from America to gussy up King Louis's court."

"I was?"

Reggie slapped him heartily on the back and said, "Don't go gettin' stars in your eyes. They wasn't lookin' at you, lad. They couldn't take their eyes off her." He pointed to Amanda. "She's a natural-born star. I don't know what makes a man or a woman a star, but it's something you can't learn."

"Nobody noticed when I came on stage," Fargo said, "but they all did when Amanda entered."

"That's part of it. Unless I miss my guess, folks perk up and pay attention when you walk into a saloon. But the theater's different. You don't have to be tough, or even pretty, to be a star, though it helps if you're both."

"It's not real," Fargo protested. "The way those two fought would have made them laughingstocks in any bar fight I was ever in."

"They were playing to the audience, not fencing for real," Reggie said. "That's what is so beguiling about the stage, doing harmless things and making the audience think they're real. Now you come on along and keep me company. Miss Fredericks's got people to talk to. Fans. I have to keep most of them out, especially the drunks."

Fargo had seen waiters moving through the audience during the performance serving liquor. Those closest to the stage and in the boxes rising up on the theater walls to either side of the stage had seemed to be enjoying themselves without getting pickled. Farther back in the theater, especially the standing-room-only crowd pressed against the rear wall, had been different. Fargo was not certain if any of those patrons were sober.

He saw Amanda caught up in a crush of well-wishers and left her to bask in the glory of her triumphant first performance. Fargo had seen his share of plays, but nothing like this one. Amanda had been radiant and had seemed perfect for the role, though she could not have rehearsed even one minute before going onstage. Missing most of the play had put him at a disadvantage, but Fargo thought he had followed the story well enough to see how good Amanda Fredericks was as an actress, flawlessly delivering her lines and turning every head in the audience. She had changed personalities entirely and become the main character.

She had been the star.

"We got to let in the reporters but not the rest," Reggie said. He started to say something more, then bit back the words. Fargo saw the way the old man fingered the six-shooters shoved into his belt before going to the door. He expected trouble and was ready to shoot it out with someone. Fargo just didn't know who.

Reggie pulled back on the bar holding the stage door closed and then leaped back. Fargo thought there was an explosion outside from the way the door blasted inward. Men tumbled on top of one another, each screaming to be let in.

"None of that, fellows," Reggie said, putting himself between the writhing pile on the floor, and the dressing rooms where Amanda gathered with her admirers. "You can go in. You, the *Alta* reporter. Go on. Who're you?"

"I'm from the *Herald*, sir," a young man said, looking up. "My name's Willie Watkins, and I'd give anything for an interview with Miss Fredericks. I promise it will be the best review she's ever received. She was fabulous!"

"Gimme your left nut," Reggie said. "Doesn't look like you're using it."

"Sir?"

Fargo had to laugh at the young man and how confused he appeared. Then Fargo remembered how he had been the same way onstage, stumbling around and going where the other actors had pointed. From the green look about him, Watkins was new at the reporting job and only wanted to make good on a big interview with a newly arrived star of Amanda Fredericks's stature.

"You, the one who played King Louis's Indian! Can I get an interview with you?" Willie Watkins held out a small notebook and a pencil like an offering. It took Fargo a couple seconds to realize the reporter was talking to him.

"Go on in, Mr. Watkins," said Reggie. "You be sure to say nice things about Mr. Fargo."

"I will, since he was, uh, he was perfect as a nonspeaking aborigine of dubious origins at King Louis's court."

Reggie moved to block the several others from entering, herding them back through the door to the small landing outside the theater. Watkins hurried to Fargo, but the way the reporter's eyes kept darting backstage toward Amanda's dressing room, Fargo knew the young man only used this interview as a ploy to speak with the real star.

Willie Watkins came over, but Fargo saw the difficulty Reggie was having at the door. The reporters who had been denied entry had gone, leaving behind a rowdy bunch of drunks.

"I wanna meet her," shouted one. "She'll marry me, if'n I kin jist see her!"

The press of Amanda's adoring—and inebriated—admirers caused Fargo to push Watkins to one side and go to Reggie's aid. Together they tried to close the door, but the number of men on the other side prevented it. The door exploded inward again, sending Fargo staggering back and throwing Reggie to the floor.

The situation flashed before Fargo's eyes. Reggie was going to be trampled unless the drunken crowd was stopped, but the only way Fargo could do that was to shoot one or two of them. They threatened the old man's life with their heavy boots, but Fargo was hesitant to kill them in cold blood.

"Gentlemen, please! Quiet down!" came Amanda's lilting voice. The blonde swept out of her dressing room and held up her hand. "I wish I could talk with you all personally on this night of personal triumph, but there are so many of you."

"Thass all right. Marry me," said the drunkest of the crowd, stumbling forward to plant a slobbery kiss on her cheek. Fargo intercepted him before he could grab hold of Amanda, and sent him reeling, but the rest were oozing through the door onto the backstage like ants homing in on an open sugar bowl. If he plugged one trail, two more would open and let even more in.

"Into the theater, then!" Amanda cried. "Go back into the theater where you can sit down, and I will speak with you there!" She shot a look of resignation at Fargo, as if she wished she could do something else but her fame held her captive. In spite of that look of surrender to the inevitable, Fargo knew she was in her element and would not have chosen to be anywhere else, even with him.

As Amanda left to address her adoring throngs, Fargo helped Reggie to his feet. The old man put his hand on the butt of a pistol and looked at Fargo.

"Go protect her," he said. "My leg's hurtin' bad and I can't."

"What do you mean?" Fargo asked. Before the old man could answer, Fargo was distracted.

"Mr. Fargo," said McGuire, hurrying up and looking more than a little frightened. "Do as Reggie said, please! I can't let anything happen to Amanda. I can't! I need her."

"You need the crowds she'll draw," grumbled Reggie, sitting heavily in his chair and rubbing his leg. "You don't care a spit about her. I know you!"

47

"I don't deny that she's the best draw I've had in a year," McGuire said. "The Montgomery Street Melodeon is close to insolvency." He saw Fargo's expression and said, "I'm damned near bankrupt. Amanda's my only hope for making enough money to keep going."

"What's this about something happening to her?" asked Fargo. "The drunks are under control now. She's got quite a way about her. I'd have drilled a couple if they had kept pushing to get in, but she got them to sit down all peaceable-like."

"Tell him, you bloated toad," grumbled Reggie. "You owe it to her to hire somebody who can watch after her."

"Amanda's in danger?" Fargo's hand drifted to his Colt.

"I'm afraid she might be," McGuire said reluctantly.

Fargo saw there was more the theater owner wasn't telling, but wasting time getting it out of him might only place Amanda in more danger. Fargo pushed past McGuire and went to the wings, where he could see Amanda holding court in the center of the stage, and fifty or more onlookers in the impromptu audience hooting and calling at her. She put on a one-woman show, reciting lines from plays Fargo could not identify and showing a bit of leg now and then to the great approval of her admirers. McGuire's waiters wasted no time selling whiskey to the crowd, taking their money and getting them even drunker. Fargo hoped they would pass out soon, but saw no sign of that happening.

Fargo almost turned to grab McGuire by the lapels and force him to tell what was going on when a sixth sense warned him of danger. Fargo's sharp eyes scanned the audience and saw nothing, but his sense of danger heightened.

"Amanda!" he shouted. He ran onto the stage, amid hoots and howls of outrage. Everything started to move as if the world had been dipped in molasses. Fargo heard Amanda say something to him as he dived, his arms wrapping around her slender waist. He hit her hard, jolting her as he knocked her to the stage.

A gunshot rang out and a bullet ripped through the set behind her.

"Skye!" she cried in protest. Then she looked back at the hole in the set. "Someone shot at me!"

Fargo scrambled to his feet and whipped out his Colt. At the rear of the theater he saw a man holding a six-shooter, aiming along the barrel for another shot. Fargo got off two quick shots in the man's direction. Both went wide of their target, but the threat of getting ventilated was enough to convince the man to hightail it.

Fargo jumped off the stage into the deep orchestra pit, and scrambled out of it to give chase. He found himself buffeted about by the drunks in the audience, all trying to get out of the theater. By the time he forced himself through the stumbling, pushing crowed of men and reached the rear of the theater, the gunman was long gone.

While he could have given chase, Fargo decided protecting Amanda was more important. He returned to the stage, jumped, and pulled himself up. Amanda stood with Reggie in the wings. The doorman had both pistols drawn and looked determined to use them, should anyone threaten Amanda again.

"Where's McGuire?" Fargo demanded.

"Skye, don't leave me," pleaded Amanda. "I've gotten bad reviews before, but nothing like this. No one's ever shot at me while I was onstage!"

"I want to find out why someone did tonight," Fargo said, prying loose her fingers to go after Horatio McGuire. As he left he heard Reggie assuring her that the gunman was not a critic but only one of the drunks who had gotten a bit too enthusiastic.

Fargo wished that were so, but he knew better. The ambusher had not been drunk. His hand had been steady as he aimed, and he had not run off as if he had been hitting the bottle too hard. From the few words Fargo had with McGuire before the shooting, he knew the theater owner feared something more than the random disorder of too many men in a city with too few women.

He found Horatio McGuire huddled behind a stack of scenery left over from some earlier play. The man looked up fearfully as Fargo approached.

"Is it over?"

"She could have been killed," Fargo accused. "You knew it was going to happen. Who's trying to kill Amanda?"

"I . . . I don't know," he lied.

Fargo stepped up, towered over the corpulent theater owner and looked like doom descending. He did not even have to rest his hand on the butt of his holstered pistol to get the man talking.

"All right, all right. I worried that something like this might happen. But I didn't know. Th-they're awful men and will do anything, but I didn't think they would try to kill a woman."

"Who're you talking about?"

"The Sydney Ducks," McGuire said. "They run San Francisco. Every policeman is on the take—and gets bribes from the Ducks. They are moving into extortion. They told me they would shut down my melodeon if I didn't pay them a hundred dollars a week. In gold!"

"Did you pay them?"

"I don't have the money. Desirée wasn't bringing in the crowds I needed to pay them. That was why I let Amanda go on tonight. She's a star. The audience loved her. I'll pack 'em in for months. I don't want her harmed!"

"It's foolish for these Ducks to shoot at her if that's the only way you'll be able to pay them their money," Fargo pointed out.

"They don't know or care about show business. They wanted to scare me."

Fargo started to say that they had succeeded, but held his tongue.

"You can't pay extortion money," he said instead.

"I know. I'm not making enough to cover salaries and rent on the theater!"

"That's not what I meant. You pay them, you make them stronger. You have to stand up to them."

"They'll kill me." When McGuire saw this didn't do much to convince Fargo, he added, "And anyone working here. That means Amanda."

"She can get a job at some other theater. The Bella Union, maybe."

McGuire reacted as if he had thrust his hand into fire.

"She can't go there! They're a bunch of crooks! They'll use her and never pay!"

"Like you were intending to do?" Fargo asked, taking a shot in the dark. From McGuire's expression, he knew he had hit the man's intentions dead center. McGuire wanted Amanda to bring in the crowds, he would use the money to pay off his bills, and then force her to either keep performing in the hope of collecting her back pay or leave and lose what she had earned.

"She's renegotiating her contract," Fargo said. "She gets paid at the end of every performance. You don't pay, she leaves."

"You can't do that!"

"I'll see to the Sydney Ducks," Fargo said. "I've butted heads with them already and they don't look that tough."

"You're wrong, Fargo, you're wrong," McGuire said.

"I won't be dead wrong." Fargo turned and went to find Amanda. Reggie had herded her into her secluded dressing room where she would be safe. As he walked across the empty stage, he heard a soft chuckling from the darkened theater.

Fargo stopped, turned, and looked out over the now empty seats. The chuckle turned to mocking laughter that echoed from one side to the other. He reached for his six-shooter. He drew the gun, went into a crouch, and aimed directly for one of the box seats above him at stage left. A dim figure stood there.

The man stepped forward enough for Fargo to identify him.

"Nance!"

Calling Clay Nance's name caused the man to disappear like a prairie dog down his burrow. Fargo lit out, going into the far wings and around until he found a spiral staircase leading to that box. He paused at the curtain, gripped his six-shooter tighter, and then burst in.

Empty. Fargo leaned over the railing on the balcony and saw Nance below, heading out of the theater.

"Stop!" he shouted, knowing that he wouldn't. Fargo

vaulted the low railing and fell ten feet to land heavily in front of the rows of chairs in the main theater. He got his feet under him and sprinted for the lobby as the outer door swung shut.

Fargo got to the steps leading to the theater in time to see the fog swallow Nance like some swirling, vaporous beast devouring its dinner. Walking slowly in the direction Nance had taken, Fargo warily sought the fleeing man. Within two blocks he knew he was on a fool's errand. The Sydney Duck had disappeared into the fog without a trace.

7

Fargo shivered as the clammy fog slipped wetly against his face and hands. He turned in a full circle, every sense alert. He heard distant noises from the bay. Ships creaked against their moorings and from deeper in the city came sounds of people moving about lightheartedly. Fargo was not certain where McGuire's Montgomery Street Melodeon lay in relation to other theaters, but it could not be too far away. Such establishments tended to cluster together.

He took a few tentative steps in the direction he thought Clay Nance had gone, then stopped. Not even the Trailsman could find someone in this thick fog. Nance would have left no tracks on the wet pavement, and he knew San Francisco's alleys and back streets better than Fargo did.

Resigned, Fargo retraced his steps to McGuire's theater and went into the lobby. The entire theater seemed alien to him now, a strange territory that had turned deadly. Fargo knelt and looked at the spot where the gunman had fired at Amanda while she was onstage. He had not expected to find any blood, and he didn't. He did find where one of his own bullets had dug a hole in the wall near the gunman.

Fargo wound around inside the theater and got up into the box where Clay Nance had stood. He examined the floor and seats of the balcony box seats, but found nothing worth a second glance.

Disgusted at his lack of progress, Fargo returned to the stage and slipped behind the curtains, making his way to Amanda's dressing room. Amanda sat on a short cot, a towel over her face.

"Is she—?" he started, worrying that the blonde had been hurt.

McGuire put his pudgy finger to his lips, cautioning Fargo to silence. He motioned him out of the tiny dressing room.

"She's fine," McGuire said. His eyes darted about nervously. Fargo thought of a cornered animal trying to find a way to escape. "She's resting now. The strain. Nerves. It has been horrible for her, you know."

"It's going to be horrible for you if you don't tell me how to stop the Sydney Ducks," Fargo said. "If it takes grabbing you by your ankles, holding you upside down, and shaking until money falls out, I'll do it. Or I might just advise Amanda to leave."

"No!" The panicked expression on McGuire's face told Fargo how desperate the theater owner was to keep Amanda working on his stage.

"You're going to tell me everything I need to know. Start with Clay Nance."

"You know him? He's a leader of the Ducks. Not the biggest, but one of them who—"

"I don't care about that," snapped Fargo. "Is he the one shaking you down?" Fargo saw the answer on McGuire's face. "There's more than extortion going on, isn't there? You could hire an army of toughs to protect both Amanda and your theater for less than what Nance would squeeze out of you."

"You're right, Fargo," McGuire said reluctantly. "It's not just extortion money. Not exactly. It's more like I borrowed money from him."

"So Nance—and the Sydney Ducks—loaned you money to keep the theater open," Fargo said.

"But they are charging exorbitant interest! I can barely keep my head above water. It's terrible!"

Fargo saw that McGuire had to deal with Nance eventually on the matter of the borrowed money, but that did not excuse having gunmen shoot at McGuire's star. Fargo took it personally that Nance or anyone else would try to harm Amanda.

"I'll see what I can do," Fargo said.

"Whatever you do, don't go to the police," warned McGuire. "They're worse than the Ducks."

Fargo remembered what he had been told earlier about corruption in the police force.

"I'll tell Nance I'm speaking for you. If you don't go along with whatever I work out with him, I'll make sure Amanda is gone in a flash."

"I could always put Desirée back onstage," McGuire mused, then saw his ploy was not working. He had already admitted the temperamental Desirée Lefanu wasn't drawing the crowds Amanda could.

"You see Miss Fredericks back to the hotel when she wakes up," Fargo said. "I'll let you know what Nance says about easing up on demanding repayment from you."

Fargo had no idea where to find Clay Nance, other than at Larson's Lair. The pimp Bangers was another possible source of information, although Fargo didn't see that he could get anything important from that man. Going to the Sydney Ducks' hangout and watching for an opportune moment to press his case was Fargo's best course of action. After he had gotten a feel for the ebb and flow at the saloon, he would have a better notion of what to do.

He did not want to shoot it out with Clay Nance. Killing the man would solve nothing because another member of the cutthroat gang would take his place in demanding the loan repayment. There probably wasn't any secret about Horatio McGuire owing the Ducks money.

Fargo marched through the fog-cloaked San Francisco streets and watched as a small breeze blowing off the bay pushed away the worst of the mist. He had a feeling that it was nearing sunrise because of the change in winds off the Pacific. Fargo yawned and kept walking, wanting to sleep, but wanting to settle accounts with Nance and the Ducks even more.

He found Larson's Lair as the sun poked up above the bay, giving pale light to the dingy street. Fargo had not realized the entire area around Sydney-Town was so garbage strewn and disreputable looking. The buildings had cracked, peeling paint and in places the wood was eaten away, either by rot or worms.

He dodged tight groups of men going toward the saloon,

but saw nothing of Clay Nance. Fargo watched the front of the saloon from an alcove across the street, unsure of what to do. Barging in again would draw more than a little trouble from the bouncer he had beaten up on his prior entrance.

For all he knew, Nance might decide to take a shot or two at him for siding with McGuire.

As he watched, a small knot of blue-uniformed men strolled along the street. A tiny gold badge flashed on one's chest as he turned and looked around the street. The policeman went into the saloon but came out again less than a minute later. He spoke with the other four coppers, then waved them to follow him. Fargo saw them turn the corner and disappear.

He let out a lungful of air he had not even known he was holding in. But Fargo saw no one else go into or come out of Larson's Lair over the next half hour. There was a time for patience and a time for boldness. Fargo crossed the street and went to the door.

He put his hand on his Colt, then started into Larson's Lair when a sharp voice from down the street froze him in his tracks.

"You there. Whatcha doing?"

"Fargo saw the group of policemen rushing down the street toward him. He relaxed and stepped away from the saloon entrance. He had been uncertain about involving the police, but they were dealing themselves into the game.

The police fanned out in a half circle around him when the leader stepped up, chin thrust out belligerently.

"You ain't go no call goin' in there. That's a private club and you ain't no member."

"You know all the, uh, members?" Fargo asked. He felt his hackles rising.

"Who are you?"

"I work for Horatio McGuire," Fargo said, stretching the truth a little. He wanted to solve the theater owner's problems because they were also Amanda's, but he did not get paid by McGuire for his work.

"You wouldn't be named Fargo, now would you?"

The way the police officer said his name told Fargo he

was in deep trouble. There was no way he could shoot his way out facing so many men. Two of the coppers tapped blackjacks against their palms. Two more slapped polished clubs against their thighs, as if they were judging distances from their clubs to the top of Fargo's head.

"Who are you?" Fargo asked.

"I'm Hayworth, the leader of this band of Specials. We get paid for keepin' the peace any way we can."

Fargo had heard of them. Technically not police working for the city and citizens of San Francisco, they sold their services to the highest bidder. The regular police deferred to them and their often illegal ways. Fargo came to a quick decision as to who paid for this group of Specials. He had seen Hayworth go into Larson's Lair earlier.

Fargo reacted without conscious thought. He stepped forward and pushed both hands hard against the officer's chest, sending him stumbling back into two other Specials. The others came at him, but Fargo wasn't sticking around to let them bash in his skull. He ducked, twisted around, and dived through the door into Larson's Lair. Hitting the floor belly-down, he wiggled a few feet and got his feet under him.

The few Sydney Ducks in the saloon stirred sleepily. The barkeep sat bolt upright from where he slept on the bar, his hand going for a knife. Fargo shoved him off the bar. He landed hard on the floor and broke a couple of bottles of cheap whiskey as he fell.

The noise and commotion distracted the Specials coming after Fargo—for a few seconds. He used the time well and raced for the back of the saloon. There had to be a back door. A gang of outlaws like the Sydney Ducks wouldn't let themselves get bottled up without an escape path. He found it at the back of the storage room.

The door leading to the rear alley was barred, but Fargo yanked the locking rod off. He got the door open and took off down the alley. He heard whistles blowing frantically as he burst out into the next street over from the Ducks' hangout. Dawn roused the city, and merchants already moved about, opening their shops for another day's business and taking deliveries from other tradesmen.

Fargo slowed his breakneck pace and tried to blend in with the crowd in the street. He didn't get twenty yards before a knot of three Specials spotted him and blew an alert on their whistles.

He started for a store, only to have someone in the street trip him. He hit the ground hard and then was pinned down before he could move. A Special held one leg and two more grabbed his arms. When they pulled him to his feet, he faced the officer he had shoved.

"Assaultin' a peace officer," Hayworth growled. "Take him to the lockup. Don't be too gentle with the son of a bitch!"

Fargo was kicked and cuffed all the way down the street to a storefront that had been converted into a police station. Inside sat four more Specials.

"We got a live one for you," Hayworth said. "Put him on ice."

"Right away," answered a Special with a ring of keys dangling at his belt. Fargo let him push him toward the rear of the dingy office and through a narrow door. Doors to four empty cells stood open.

Fargo heard a commotion behind him in the office, then silence. He realized he could never get out of the iron cages—and he suspected that what was being said back in the office concerned him and his future good health.

"Oh, oh," he moaned, clutching his belly. He doubled up and fell heavily to the floor. "They must have busted something inside."

"You sluggard," the jailer said, coming over to kick Fargo in the ribs. As he reared back to deliver the blow, Fargo rolled into him, knocking him over like a tenpin. The jailer's arms flailed about as he tried to keep his balance, then he crashed to the floor with Fargo surging up on top of him. Fargo gauged his distance and punched short and hard. The turnkey's head snapped back and all the fight went out of him.

Fargo grabbed the man's six-shooter and shoved it into his empty holster, then went to listen at the door leading back into the office. He recognized Clay Nance's voice instantly.

"I pay you gents more 'n enough for a little chore like this."

"But murder, Mr. Nance. That's what it is."

"Murder is such a strong word, mate. Consider how that bloke broke free and tried to escape. Why, bloody hell, he was a dangerous one and shot one of your men. Don't ya care about your men, Hayworth? Or are you too busy plottin' to take my position with the Ducks?"

The unexpected gunshot caused Fargo to jump. The deathly silence told him Nance had fired the shot to emphasize his control.

"Now that's a bloody shame, it is, me puttin' a hole in your bloody damn hat," Nance said cheerfully. "Which of you fine, upstanding lawmen is going to win a reward by bringing down the escaping prisoner who might just murder one of your number?"

Fargo knew he had only seconds before the Specials crowded into the cell block to kill him. He knelt, got his arms under the jailer's arm and hoisted him as a shield as the door opened. Fargo shoved the turnkey's corpse into the office, taking the Specials by surprise. Hayworth stepped back, a look of black rage clouding his face. Fortunately for Fargo, the hatred was directed at Nance.

Fargo fired twice as he vaulted over the pile of them and got out the door and into the street.

He turned and fired until the six-shooter came up empty, trying to keep the Specials bottled up.

Running hell-bent for leather down the street, Fargo cut down side streets and alleys and finally saw a wagon creaking along under the burden of its cargo. He grabbed the tarp covering the crates in the wagon bed and jumped into the wagon, pulling the canvas down over him. Peering out under the edge of the tarp, Fargo saw a dozen blue-coated Specials converge from all directions. He fingered the six-shooter he had taken from the jailer and knew he had emptied its cylinder.

But the Specials paid the wagon no heed as it rattled over the wood-plank streets and onto dirt as it left Sydney-Town.

Fargo had no idea where it went, but he saw fewer and fewer Specials until the only people he saw were Chinese.

"What you do there?" came the shrill question. "You get out. Now!"

The tarp was yanked back. Fargo looked up and saw the driver of the wagon was a Celestial. The man looked angry that Fargo had hitched a ride without telling him.

"I'm sorry if I've caused you any trouble," Fargo said.

"You go, you go now!"

Fargo hesitated, then said, "Let me repay your kindness by helping unload your wagon."

"You want money. You no get! You go, you go!"

Fargo got to his feet and lifted a heavy crate. "Where do you want me to put his?"

The Chinaman stared at him for a moment, then silently pointed. Fargo got down from the wagon and stacked the crate next to a dozen others, then returned and began working to unload the rest. He figured the driver would tell him if any were not intended for unloading there.

The Celestial stood with arms crossed, watching Fargo work until all the crates were removed from the wagon.

"Why you do that?"

"I was getting away from the Specials," Fargo said, not wanting to varnish the truth. "You saved my neck by coming along when you did. It wasn't fair of me to put you at risk. If the Specials had found me, they might have thought you were willingly helping me."

The Celestial stood for a few seconds, stared at Fargo with dark, unfathomable eyes, then spat.

"Specials," he said. Then he ground his slippered foot down on the spittle. "They no come to Chinatown. You safe here."

The Celestial bowed slightly. Fargo wasn't sure what to do so he duplicated the bow.

"Thank you for allowing me to help you," Fargo said, pointing to the heavy crates. He wondered if there had been others who would have helped this man if he had not done the unloading himself. The Chinaman was old, frail, and hardly looked strong enough to stand up, much less pick up any of the heavy boxes.

"You go, you go now," the Chinaman said firmly. As Fargo turned, the man called after him, "You need work, you ask for Wo Lin!"

8

The doorman opened the plate-glass door leading into the lobby for Fargo, but this time the uniformed man gave a look of disdain because of his condition. Fargo had been crawling through filth and getting shot at and otherwise brushing shoulders with the angel of death, and sorely needed to clean himself up.

"Is Miss Fredericks in her room?" Fargo asked.

The doorman hesitated, then shook his head.

Fargo took the steps leading to the second floor two at a time and threw open Amanda's door. Empty. The bed had not been slept in. He went to the wardrobe and opened the door. While he did not remember every dress the actress had, he thought many were missing. Fargo turned to the dresser and sucked in his breath. Combs and other personal items were definitely missing. He remembered seeing them spread out in a precise manner on the dresser top.

As much as he needed another bath, he had to find out what had happened to the woman. Fargo went to his room, got ammunition for the pistol he had taken off the Special jailer, then left the hotel in a hurry.

He went directly to the Montgomery Street Melodeon and rattled the front doors. They were securely chained and no amount of knocking brought anyone to let him in. Fargo circled the building to the stage door and rapped sharply on it.

"Reggie? Are you there? It's me. It's Fargo!" He hammered on the door some more, but got no response."

Stepping back, Fargo looked up and saw four stories of sheer red brick. He had hoped to find a window and enter that way. The longer it took him to get into the theater, the more anxious he became. McGuire had promised to take

Amanda back to the hotel. He obviously had not. Fargo had to find what had gone awry.

The only way he could get to the roof was up a drainpipe at the corner of the huge building. Fargo spit on his hands, jumped onto a rain barrel, and then began shinning up. When he was almost to the top the pipe began to pull free from the wall. Fargo leaned in toward the wall and tried to shift the direction his weight pulling on the drainpipe. When he saw this wasn't going to work, he scrambled frantically for the last few feet. His fingers clutched at the brick edging as the pipe pulled free.

Fargo found himself dangling by his fingertips, kicking futilely against the brick wall. He calmed down when he realized he was going to take a long fall if he didn't get over the verge fast. Fargo moved his feet slowly until he kicked free some mortar from between bricks and won himself a little toehold. This took some pressure off his fingers and let him straighten enough to get a better grip on the roof. A deep breath, a sudden exhalation, and a concerted effort of legs and hands propelled him over the edge and onto the sloping roof. He lay flat, panting for breath until he got his strength back.

Fargo sidled around and looked down almost three stories to the alley. Falling from here would have given him more than a jolt. It might have broken every bone in his body.

His boots slipped on the shingled roof, but he moved cautiously until he reached the top of the slope, and looked out over three more peaks. The rooftop had been built in sections and looked like a cantilever bridge. But Fargo was less concerned about how the rain flowed off the roof than he was with the trapdoor he had just spotted. He scrambled down the far side of the slope and caught the edge of the door. He wasn't too surprised that it was unlocked.

Fargo opened it, flipped through and dropped a few feet onto a rickety catwalk. He looked over the stage thirty feet below and into the quiet, dark theater. Fargo made his way along the narrow board catwalk until he reached a ladder going down into the wings. He dropped the last few feet.

The sound of his boots hitting the floor sent echoes throughout the deathly still theater.

Fargo drew his six-shooter and cautiously went to Amanda's dressing room. The door stood ajar. He pushed it open with the pistol barrel and saw her lying on the narrow cot.

With a rush, he entered the room, spun around, and aimed his cocked six-gun at the man behind the door.

"Don't shoot!" Reggie said, eyes going wide with fear.

"What's going on?" asked Amanda, stirring. She rubbed the sleep from her gray eyes as she sat up.

"You were supposed to go back to the hotel. Why did you stay here?" Fargo lowered his six-shooter, but continued to stare at Reggie. The old man pushed his two guns back into his belt.

"Mr. McGuire thought it was too dangerous venturing out on the streets, even with Reggie guarding me. So I decided to stay here. Reggie was good enough to stay, also, after he fetched some of my clothing and toiletries from the hotel."

"That's the way it is, Fargo," Reggie said. "I figured you'd show up eventually."

"The doors are all locked," Fargo said. "How was I supposed to get in?"

"You're here, ain't you?" Reggie asked, getting back some of his vinegar. "The best place for me to watch over Miss Fredericks was here, not back at the stage door."

"She's mighty pretty, isn't she?" asked Fargo in a voice low enough for only Reggie to hear. The old man's smile told the story. Here he could savor her beauty while guarding her. Back at the hotel he would have been relegated to standing guard in the hallway, if the management even allowed that.

"I have slept in worse places, Skye," she said, stretching. Fargo sucked in his breath at the sight of her breasts flattening as her arms went high over her head. Her blonde hair was in delightful disarray, and he doubted he had ever seen her look lovelier. It was probably a good thing Reggie was still here or Fargo would have considered taking Amanda up on the rain check she had offered after the first time they'd made love. As it was, Fargo felt uneasy about her safety knowing Nance and the rest of the Sydney Ducks were intent on killing her.

"Where's McGuire? I want to talk to him," Fargo said.

"If that worthless bag of suet ain't in his office, I don't know where he would be," Reggie said.

"You keep an eye peeled," Fargo said.

"Wait, Skye. What's happened? You went off so fast after I was shot at, I didn't have a chance to ask who fired. Was it only a drunk?" Amanda looked concerned but not upset. She had no idea how McGuire had entangled her in his web of financial dealings.

"McGuire will explain it—after I find him," Fargo promised. He walked out onto the darkened stage and remembered how he had felt being an extra. So many people out there had been looking at him. It seemed distant now and more than a little unnatural, but in that instant he understood what drew Amanda to the theater.

She was a lovely woman and had, for a brief moment, held everyone in the theater in her sway. They hung on her words, followed her movements, and would have killed for her if she had asked. That kind of heady power could be addictive.

Fargo stepped forward and started to speak—to find out what it would be like. Then he realized he had sampled as much of the lure of the stage as he was ever likely to. This was not for him.

He walked off the stage to the narrow passage going behind the spiral stairs leading to the box seats in the balconies along the walls, beginning to worry. There were too many places for a sniper to hide for him ever to protect Amanda if she were onstage. He found a flight of steps up into the mezzanine above the huge lobby. He looked down and saw only emptiness. But from an office a few yards farther he heard McGuire mumbling and grumbling.

Fargo opened the door ans saw the corpulent theater owner sitting behind his desk, stacks of money in front of him. It took McGuire a few seconds to realize someone else was in his office. A pudgy hand grabbed for a small pistol to one side.

"Don't," Fargo said sharply. "I'm not going to rob you."

"Mr. Fargo," sighed McGuire, relaxing. He started to sweep the money into his desk drawer, then realized Fargo had already seen the night's gate.

"You sold a lot of tickets," Fargo said. "Amanda is a real draw."

"The best this tired old theater's ever seen," McGuire said. "But all this is accounted for. It goes for rent and supplies and—"

"Don't bother," Fargo said, cutting him off. "Do you remember what I told you about Amanda? She gets her pay at the end of every performance—off the top."

"But the Ducks! They want their blood money. Licensing fees, they call it, but it's nothing but extortion."

"If you have to pay them to keep Amanda safe for the time being, you'll do that next," Fargo said. He hated the idea of giving in to crooks, but Amanda was going to perform. He could not stop her—and he could not protect her in this rambling, many-leveled theater. The best Fargo could do at the moment was to get McGuire to buy him some time until he could deal with Clay Nance.

"I can't pay you anything," McGuire protested.

Fargo shrugged it off. He had not asked for a salary.

"I am going to plaster San Francisco with broadsides advertising Amanda's new play. *Richelieu* is well past its heyday. She is ready to go with *East Lynne* right away. We'll have a huge opening, the likes of which San Francisco has never before seen!"

Fargo let McGuire ramble on with his pipe dream of acclaim and probably fortune, as well. The theater owner had a legion of problems to deal with, getting a new show on the boards so quickly.

And Fargo has the pleasurable chore of being Amanda's bodyguard.

"Never saw the fat galoot move so fast," Reggie marvelled. "McGuire's pulled everything together in a single day."

"What about rehearsals?" grumbled an actor whose name

Fargo had failed to catch. The man danced around on his toes and made fluttery movements with his hands, as if he might take to flight at any instant. "How can he possibly expect us to put on a decent performance without *any* rehearsal?"

"You know your part, don't you?" asked Fargo.

"Of course I do!"

"Then I don't see the problem. If everyone else knows what to say, then just say it."

"Oh, you ignorant bumpkin. It's ever so much more complicated than that." The actor sniffed, put his nose up in the air and stormed off.

"Don't bother askin' my opinion of him, Fargo," said Reggie. "He's a bigger prima donna than any of the women. He's upset about not getting top billing."

Fargo wondered if the Ducks were the only ones likely to take a shot at Amanda. Most of the cast resented her premature appearance, not to mention the shortened run of *Richelieu*, which had their names on the marquee and not hers.

Amanda flitted around among the cast, speaking with them, making gestures and demands regarding how they were to do their parts.

"Isn't the director supposed to do all that?" Fargo asked, pointing at Amanda. "She seems to be taking over."

"With McGuire the way he is when it comes to Miss Fredericks, no director's gonna cross her." Reggie shook his head. "I reckon she knows more about theater than the rest of them combined. The fellow who directed McGuire's other plays didn't know squat."

"Do you think he might take it out on her?" Fargo asked, suddenly more worried about the cast and crew than the Sydney Ducks.

Reggie laughed. "He'd die of fright if he ever picked up a real gun or knife. No, if he wanted to get back at her, he'd cut down on her lines. That's his notion of revenge."

The nearer it got to curtain time, the more uneasy Fargo became. He had heard repeatedly from McGuire that ticket sales were brisk and that the Montgomery Street Melodeon was going to sell out on opening night for the first time.

Throughout the afternoon Fargo had kept a close eye on Amanda, but had seen nothing threatening.

"You got stage jitters, that's all," Reggie told him. The old man pulled his chair closer to the stage door, checked the bar he used to hold it closed, and then sat down. His two six-shooters were shoved into his broad leather belt. He rocked back and rested his hands on the butts.

"Bring 'em on," Reggie declared.

The words had barely left his mouth when a shrill scream of terror rang through the theater. Most of the actors ignored it. Some looked around, then checked their scripts. But Fargo recognized the real fear in the scream. No actress was good enough to sound that afraid—and he knew the wail had come from Amanda's dressing room.

He shoved through the crowd of actors and got to her door. He kicked it open to see her cowering back against the far wall. She made tiny choked sounds and pointed to her dressing table. A hatbox there jerked and shifted, as if it had come alive.

"What happened?" asked Fargo.

"Th-that thing!" Amanda was so frightened she could not speak.

Fargo went to the table, pulled his six-shooter and used the muzzle to flip open the lid. Peering up at him were twin red eyes filled with nothing but utter hatred for humanity. Fargo instinctively pulled the trigger and fired point-blank into the huge black rat.

A single bullet was not enough to end the life of the snapping, struggling wharf rat. Fargo fired a second time. This bullet shattered the rat's spine. It kicked feebly, glared one last time at Fargo, and then finally died.

"Is it . . . is it dead?" Amanda gasped.

Fargo dropped the lid back into the box to cover the carcass. The rat had to weigh ten pounds and could have given a terrier a fierce fight.

"Where did the hatbox come from?" Fargo asked.

"It was on my table when I got back. I thought Mr. McGuire had sent it. I . . . I opened it and saw that *thing*!"

"It's dead," Fargo said, holding her trembling body close. She sobbed, then sniffed and pushed away.

"Thank you, Skye. I shouldn't have acted like that. It was only a m-m-mouse, after all."

"Mouse, my sainted aunt," grumbled Reggie. "That wharf rat coulda ripped out your throat or bit off a finger. I seen 'em do even worse down on the docks."

"Get it out of here," Fargo said. Reggie griped as he gathered the box, now dripping with the rat's blood, and carried it from Amanda's dressing room. "Are you all right?" Fargo asked the blonde actress.

"The show must go on." Amanda tried to sound brave, but he heard real fear in her voice.

"I'll make sure it never happens again," he said.

"You know who did this?" Her gray eyes went wide in surprise.

"Get ready for your debut," Fargo told her.

"Yes, yes," muttered Amanda, but her eyes kept returning to the pool of sticky blood on her dressing table.

Fargo left her. Outside Amanda's dressing room, his eyes locked instantly with Desirée Lefanu's. The other actress sneered at him as he went up to her. The sneer vanished when Fargo reached out and shoved her back against a brick wall.

"Why did you put that rat in her dressing room?" he asked.

"What makes you think I did it?" Desirée asked. Then she saw there was no way she was going to convince Fargo it had been anyone else's doing. The shock of him shoving her wore off and a bit of braggadocio returned. "She stole my leading role!"

"You'd let a rival get bit by a wharf rat?"

"Why not? What she did to me is no worse."

Fargo wasn't going to threaten Desirée. He ought to turn her over to the police, but from what he had seen of the private Specials, he doubted the civil authorities were much better. Besides, what crime had she really committed? Frightening another woman? Amanda had not been hurt.

"You'll wish I had thrown you into a pit of those hungry rats if you try anything like this again," Fargo said.

"You talk big. You won't do anything to me!"

Fargo's blue eyes locked with Desirée's. She tried to stare him down and then averted her gaze.

"Might have gone a bit too far trying to scare her off," Desirée mumbled. "But that was all I intended. If she leaves, I get the lead back. I'm sure of it."

"If the theater goes bankrupt, nobody has a job—you included," Fargo said. "You don't have to like Amanda, but she's the only chance Horatio McGuire has of saving this theater. You give her all the support you can and stop trying to scare her."

"I don't have to like her," Desirée said like a petulant child. "I've been relegated to a minor role when I should be the star!"

"Help make the play a success and it won't matter," Fargo said. "You'll all be the talk of San Francisco. You might even get some revenge on Amanda if the critics give you a better review than her."

Desirée sniffed, then pushed past him and went to the wings. She stood with her arms crossed and muttered constantly to herself. Fargo wondered if she might try to harm Amanda but could not decide. By tipping her hand the way she had, Desirée had taken away any surprise she might have enjoyed if she really intended to hurt Amanda.

That was cold comfort to Fargo. He had one more to watch as he tried to keep Amanda alive. He went back into Amanda's dressing room and closed the door.

"Skye, darling, will you finish lacing up my dress? Good, thank you," Amanda said. Any trace of fright was gone. She had applied makeup carefully and looked ready to whip her weight in wildcats.

"The curtain goes up in a few minutes. Good—"

"No!" Amanda said, putting her hand over his mouth. "You never wish an actress that. Break a leg. That's what you say."

"All right," Fargo said, amazed at uncovering such a silly

superstition among the troupe. "Break one of those long, luscious legs of yours."

"You're a dear," she said. Amanda started to kiss him, then heard McGuire announcing the play. She turned and rushed out onto stage as the curtain went up to thunderous applause.

Fargo never got a chance to watch Amanda's performance. He was too busy watching the audience for any sign of a killer.

9

Fargo listened to the play with half an ear after his worry over what Desirée might do lessened. The dark-haired actress tried to get Amanda to muff her lines, but this seemed the extent of her viciousness now that her wharf rat had not scared her rival away. The ebb and flow in the audience worried Fargo more. He saw no way to keep an eye on everyone. There were too many out there.

He kept looking up at the box seats on either side of the stage, remembering Clay Nance had been in one. The patrons tonight were to be respectable folks, men with well-dressed ladies who might even have been their wives. McGuire had hoped the mayor of San Francisco and his wife would attend. The burgeoning social circle in the city dictated which play to attend, and which to avoid. If Amanda drew the right crowd on her opening night, the survival of McGuire's theater might be assured.

Whether it was the right people watching, Fargo could not say. There were certainly too many of them for his comfort. If Amanda felt the least bit nervous that another killer might be waiting to get her in his sights, she did not show it.

By the tumultuous end of the play, Fargo was a bundle of nerves. Amanda received a bouquet of flowers and accolades from the appreciative audience.

Fargo drifted back as the actors took their final bow and left the stage. Amanda was breathless and as lovely as ever, in spite of two hours of acting. Reggie tugged at Fargo's sleeve, drawing him to one side.

"The newsmen are going to be banging at the door any second no. What do you want to do?"

"Protect her," Fargo said. Then he smiled. "If I kept the reporters out, who'd protect me from her?"

"Good point, Fargo," Reggie said, laughing. "She lives for the stage damned near as much as she does for the good review."

The rest of Reggie's words were drowned out by the loud banging and calls from outside the stage door. Fargo glanced at Amanda and saw she was ready for the onslaught. He went to the door, yanked back the locking bar and stood back. The reporters rushed in, like the ocean into the bottom of a ship with a hole in the hull.

Fargo grabbed one or two men and swung them around, pinning them against the wall. It was obvious they were not reporters, but rather men from the audience intent only on meeting the lovely blonde star of the newest San Francisco sensation.

"Gentlemen, please, I'll speak with you all!" cried Amanda. "You first," she said, pointing to an astounded Willie Watkins. The young reporter babbled out an inane question that Amanda gracefully considered, and then she answered what would have been a far better query about the play and her role in it.

Fargo skirted the throng and went to where Desirée Lefanu stood, arms crossed over her chest and her jaw set. She glared at Amanda.

"You were good," Fargo told her.

"What difference does that make? *She* gets the publicity. No one will know I was even in the play!"

Fargo reached out and grabbed Watkins by the collar and dragged him back from the crowd.

"Here's another cast member to interview," Fargo told the young reporter. When he saw how reluctant Watkins was, Fargo said, "The others will have nothing but stories about Amanda Fredericks. You can get exclusives with her and the rest of the cast."

"Exclusives?" Watkins's eyes widened. "How do I do that?"

"Talk to Miss Lefanu and the others. I'll see what I can do about a private interview with Miss Fredericks," Fargo said. "After the other reporters leave to file their stories."

"But they'll get into print before me," the young reporter

protested. Then he grinned. "Getting to talk to Miss Fredericks without them elbowing me out of the way would be worth it, though." He started scribbling, flipped the page in his notebook, and began his interview with an appreciative Desirée.

"You got the touch, Fargo," said Reggie.

"Shooting rats isn't much to my liking," Fargo said. He waited until the reporters began repeating themselves. They were no longer interested in Amanda as a story as much as they were in being close to a lovely actress. Fargo acted as bodyguard then, moving between her and the reporters, slowly pushing them toward the back door. He herded them as he might sheep toward a dip, then locked the door.

"Oh, Skye, it is so exhilarating!" Amanda said, spinning around. She saw Willie Watkins standing in the hallway leading to her dressing room and hesitated.

"I promised him a few minutes alone with you." Fargo cleared his throat and said louder, "Five minutes. That's all."

"Very well." Amanda batted her long eyelashes at Watkins, then brushed past him and let him follow her like a puppy dog.

"That fella'll kill for you, Fargo," observed Reggie. "From the way she looked at him, Miss Fredericks might, too."

Fargo had to laugh, but this was more from nervous exhaustion than amusement. He was a man of action, and all he had done tonight was wait for danger. When it had not come, it had been a letdown. Welcome, true, but frustrating. Now he had to worry about the other shoe dropping. The Sydney Ducks were not going to let McGuire out of his loan and had shown how they settled disputes. All he had to do was keep Amanda from getting caught in the middle.

"What does the alley look like?" Fargo asked Reggie. The old man went out, twisted his grizzled head around, then looked up as if expecting the Sydney Ducks to fall from the sky, before coming back inside.

"All clear," Reggie announced. "A bit of fog forming, but otherwise, the streets are empty of traffic. Reckon most folks have gone to grab a bite to eat or have gone home."

"A good idea on both scores," Fargo said. He went to Amanda's door and knocked, then opened it. Willie Watkins jumped back guiltily, as if he had done something wrong.

"Time to go, Miss Fredericks," Fargo said. "And you need to write a story." He looked pointedly at Watkins.

"Yes, sir," Watkins said, running off like a scalded dog. Fargo frowned as he looked at the reporter's back.

"What got into him?"

"Oh, nothing, nothing," Amanda said airily. "I am so tired, Skye. So very tired after this delightful evening. But I'm also excited. I don't think I'll ever get to sleep tonight."

She came to him and ran her long fingers up and down his chest.

"Let's go back to the hotel. It's easier to watch over you there," Fargo said.

"I'd like you to do that," Amanda said, licking her lips as she stared boldly at him. "All night long."

By the time they reached the back door Reggie had hailed a cab for them. Fargo helped the woman into the carriage, then sat beside her. The fog was beginning to swirl again, brushing cold fingers of mist across his face. Amanda snuggled closer as they took off.

Fargo found a blanket on the carriage floor and pulled it up over Amanda's lap. She hastily spread the blanket so they could share it. Then her hands began moving along his leg, over his thigh and to his crotch.

"My, my, can we have another premier performance tonight?" she asked in a husky whisper.

As delightful as the blonde actress's hand and the promise it gave were, Fargo was still edgy about the Sydney Ducks attacking her. He put his hand on hers but did not encourage her to continue.

"Later, Skye?" she asked.

"When we get back safely to the hotel."

"Oh, you're no fun," she said in disgust. Amanda turned from him and looked out into the fog. Fargo tried to see lurking figures but ended up letting his imagination run wild. He saw writhing animals, strange faces, and a myriad of things that were not there. It was a relief when they arrived at the front door of the Regent.

The doorman silently opened the door and let Amanda and Fargo in. A small gathering in the lobby put Fargo on guard, but Amanda immediately went over and greeted the men and women there as if they were old friends. The best Fargo could tell, they were representative of San Francisco's social upper crust.

He stood around awkwardly. Amanda made no move to introduce him and that suited him fine. He was not dressed the way these people were, and he had nothing to say to them. Fargo had been at the Montgomery Street Melodeon not ten feet from where the play had been presented, and he could not speak knowledgeably about any part of it. His attention had been directed elsewhere.

"Good night!" called Amanda, waving grandly to the people. Fargo waited until she had gone up the stairs alone, not wanting to start unnecessary gossip about Amanda and her roughly dressed frontiersman escort. When a decent interval had passed, Fargo hurried up to Amanda's room. He started to knock, then wondered if he ought to. Fargo knew what Amanda had meant about him watching over her all night long. It was an invitation he should have been eager to accept—and would have, any other night.

He started to walk back to his room when he heard a loud thump, followed by a muffled cry for help.

He whipped out his six-shooter and rushed down the hall. A second cry, quickly stifled, came from Amanda's room. Fargo hesitated, wondering if he would have a better shot at getting to the cause of all this trouble if he waited outside and ambushed the culprits as they tried to escape.

Less than a moment had passed, and still, nobody came from Amanda's room. Fargo made up his mind, figuring that the attackers must have been waiting inside the room for her, and had more than likely planned an alternate escape route from there.

"Amanda! Are you all right?" he called. Getting no answer, Fargo stepped back, then launched himself at the door. His shoulder hit the thick wood and splintered it, wrenching the hinges from the doorjamb. Fargo stumbled as he followed the door into the room and onto the floor.

On his belly, Fargo lifted his six-shooter and hunted for a target. The room was empty. Scrambling to his feet, Fargo saw that the bedclothes were missing. He vaulted over the bed and went to the window in time to see two men hurrying into the fog with a sheet-wrapped burden on their shoulders.

"Amanda!" he shouted. Fargo knew he could never shoot at the men without hitting the woman rolled up in sheets.

He shoved his six-gun into its holster, then clambered over the sill, hung by his fingertips, and dropped to the street. The damnable fog swallowed him up fast—and blinded him to the kidnappers' path. He trusted that they would not change direction and kept walking down the middle of the street. Once he heard the clatter of hooves on the cobblestones behind him, and jumped aside just in time to avoid being run over by a carriage.

Fargo stopped and listened hard, hoping to hear a woman's cries for help. His heart sank when he realized how effectively the fog muffled sounds. Unless Amanda was within a block or so, he would never hear her calling out.

What did draw him was the distant dinging of a buoy out in San Francisco Bay. The harbor lay along this street. If the two kidnappers were members of the Sydney Ducks, there was no reason for them to come this way. Sydney-Town lay to the north, not the east. But they had their choice of directions to take once they had Amanda out of the hotel, and they had started in this direction.

It was slim but all Fargo had to go on.

The docks loomed. He heard the creaking of a sailing ship lashed up against a pier and saw faint masts poking up out of the water. The embarcadero was shut down because of the fog, but Fargo felt the undercurrent of life along the bay shore. Sailors and longshoremen were waiting for the fog to lift so they could ready the sailing ships to leave on the morning tide.

A cold knot grew in Fargo's belly. Had Nance sold Amanda to some captain for the purposes of pleasuring a crew on their long trips around the world? Or was Nance even involved? Any sailor could have seen Amanda and taken a fancy to her beauty.

If it was only a sailor and his friend, Amanda's life was in danger after they finished with her. If some captain had ordered her kidnapped to use for his personal diversion, her fate might be far worse than simple death. She could spend months at sea as a sexual captive.

His stride lengthened as he tried to cover as much distance as possible in a short time. Fargo felt time slipping away as he frantically went down one pier, looked around, and then retraced his path to find another. On the fourth pier he heard scraping noises in front of him.

This was the first pier where he had encountered other men, but were they Amanda's kidnappers? Fargo had to find out. He ran down the pier until he thought he would go all the way across the bay. When he was sure he had come to the end, the fog parted, giving him a view of the last twenty yards of pier.

Two men struggled with lengths of chain. At their feet wriggled a long white cylinder. Fargo didn't know what else it could be other than Amanda wrapped in bed sheets.

At first he could not figure out what the two longshoremen were doing. Then he drew his six-gun and shouted, "Put up your hands!"

The men looked around wildly, spotted him, and went for pistols shoved into their belts. Fargo fired twice, missing both times. He could not back off. The men had been wrapping the heavy links of anchor chain around Amanda's feet. They were going to throw her into the bay to drown. To back off now meant her certain death.

"Skye! Help!" came the muffled cry. "I'm here. Help me!"

Fargo settled down in spite of the lead flying around his head. He was a better shot than either of the dock-wallopers. Lifting his six-shooter he aimed, squeezed, and fired. His slug caught one man in the chest. The longshoreman sat down heavily and clutched at the bloody wound.

"He got me," was all the man croaked out to his partner.

"You whore's son!" screamed the other man. He kicked hard against Amanda. Fargo fired again and missed. Then the longshoreman succeeded in rolling Amanda's chain-wrapped form off the dock. She sailed like a fluttering apparition into the dark water, landing with a loud splash before vanishing from sight.

Fargo emptied his six-shooter, but the two men were disappearing over the end of the dock. He had no time to go after them. Fargo stripped off his gun belt, and kicked off his boots before he jumped feetfirst off the dock. The cold water robbed him of breath, but Fargo knew he had only seconds to find Amanda and free her.

Kicking hard, he dived deeper into the murky water. He flailed about, blindly hunting for the bound woman. The inky depths crushed the air from his lungs, but Fargo did not give up. He kicked harder, went deeper—and his fingers closed around the fluttering linen sheet.

Bubbles escaping from his mouth, Fargo tugged at the sheet. He could not budge it. The heavy chain weighed Amanda down. Drawing his Arkansas toothpick, Fargo slashed at the cloth until Amanda's head came free. Her blonde hair floated ghostlike in the water. Her eyes were closed, and she did not respond as Fargo pulled at her arms.

He kept hacking away until the sheet was in tatters. There remained only a few turns of chain around her ankles before he freed her entirely. Lungs burning like fire, Fargo broke the surface. He gasped for air, then rolled onto his back to be sure Amanda's face stayed above water. He stroked for the pilings and found a ladder going to the top of the pier.

Fargo slung Amanda over his back and held her slender wrists with one hand while he used the other to scale the ladder. Eventually, he reached the top of the pier and dropped Amanda flat on her back.

Her breasts rose and fell, then she gasped, rolled onto her side, and coughed up water.

"Amanda, are you going to be all right?"

"Skye, I knew you'd save me. You *did* save me? I feel awful!"

Fargo left her and ran to the far side of the dock where the two men had vanished. A trail of blood led him to the far side of the pier. Below, near a piling, Fargo saw a rope floating on the water. They must have slid down the rope and escaped in a rowboat tied up there. He looked over San Francisco Bay, hoping to catch sight of the men.

The fog kept him from seeing more than a hundred feet.

Angry that the two kidnappers had escaped, Fargo went back to help Amanda to her feet. The only bright spots were that Fargo had winged one of the men and that Amanda was alive.

"Let's get out of here," he said, putting his arm around her waist to support her. She said something he did not understand, then collapsed.

Fargo picked up the blonde actress and carried her back to the hotel.

10

Fargo decided not to go in the front where the doorman would be attentively watching every move he might make. Amanda was almost naked, Fargo's frantic knife slashing having cut not only the sheet confining her, but her nightgown as well. As much as Amanda sought publicity, this was not the kind she really needed. He went to the rear doorway and climbed the stairs to the second floor. This door opened with a special key, which Fargo did not have.

He put Amanda down and used his knife again, this time to jimmy the door. Then he roused her enough to get her moving inside and down the hall to his room. He wondered how long it would be until someone noticed that Amanda's door had been kicked in. It surprised Fargo a little that all the noise earlier when he had burst into her room had not brought anyone running. Still, considering what he had done to the door, Fargo decided that they would be safer in his room.

"Oh, a bed," Amanda sighed, throwing herself facedown on it. Fargo closed the door behind him, locked it, and then heaved a sigh. It had been a hell of a night, and not one he wanted to repeat. His shoulder had begun to hurt where he had smashed down the door, and every breath felt as if he sucked in ground glass. Fargo could only guess what condition Amanda was in, though from where he stood she seemed none the worse for wear and tear.

If anything, she looked lovelier than ever, especially with the broad patches of bare white skin showing so tantalizingly through her tattered nightgown.

"So nice, so warm," Amanda murmured, snuggling into the bedding. Fargo tossed the bedspread over her and then sat in a chair, staring at her. He wished he could go to sleep like that.

Fargo was so keyed up that he jumped at every sound in the quiet hotel. It took him some time to settle down, and when he did, he felt the tug of sleep on his eyelids, too.

He kicked off his boots and began wringing the water out of his buckskins to keep himself awake.

"At least I got a chance to wash them," he said wryly. Fargo hung up the buckskins and sat back in the chair so he could guard Amanda as she slept. In this position, he had his six-shooter close at hand and could watch the actress and the door at the same time. He did not care how securely locked it was. He had seen how easy it was to get into the hotel past locked doors. Nobody would get by a few well-placed hunks of lead from his six-gun.

Thinking about his six-shooter roused him to get some ammo and reload. He would have been in a real pickle if he had tried to shoot it out again with nothing but six empty chambers. As he worked, wiping off water and reloading the cylinders, he felt the tug of sleep more and more until he finally realized he could go no farther.

Fargo tried to stretch out a little in the chair but could not. He put his six-gun on the bedside table and climbed into bed next to Amanda. She murmured something and put her arm around his bare chest. She wiggled some more and before he knew it, they were together under the blanket, their practically naked bodies pressing together.

"Night," Amanda said, rolling over to face away from him. He rolled in the same direction and slipped closer. They fit together like spoons in a kitchen drawer, and soon both slept.

Fargo was not sure how long he had been sleep when he felt stirrings in his crotch. A light, dancing touch stroked over his flaccid length, tormenting him and causing him to stiffen slowly. He was still more asleep than awake when he felt Amanda's slender leg lift and go behind his, pulling his crotch firmly into her rounded bottom.

This brought him awake. She was reaching between her legs to play with his manhood, coaxing it to full length.

"Finally got you awake, huh?" she said. Amanda tensed her leg a little and pulled him even more into her body. She reached down and caught his steely manhood and guided it into her warm, moist center.

"Feels good," he said, still coming out of the deep sleep.

"What? This?" she asked, squeezing down with her strong inner muscles, giving him a massage from the tip to the base of his hidden shaft. "Or this?" Amanda began rotating her buttocks, pressing her warm rounded flesh into the curve of Fargo's loins. Then she shoved herself backward and took him even farther into her steamy interior.

Fargo was totally awake now. He reached around and cupped her breast. He tweaked the nipple and felt it turn from rubber to a hard, pulsing little nub. Amanda cooed like a bird. She reached down and stroked over his leg, then moved back between her legs and found the hairy bag holding his family jewels.

Fargo gasped when she began stroking over the sac at the same time that she was moving her hips and keeping him so firmly clenched inside her.

"What's wrong, Skye?" she teased. "You can dish it out but you can't take it?"

"Dish it out like this?" he asked. He began shoving forward and pulling back just a little, causing him to slip in and out of her well-lubricated channel like a piston on a steam engine. Every thrust was short and powerful, building passion like a locomotive builds pressure.

"Keep doing that, oh, yes," she sighed.

He kissed the back of her neck as he played with her breasts. First the right one and then the left. Fargo made sure he did not miss a single square inch of that silky smooth skin as he stroked and tweaked and tried to remold them into a different shape. He was content with the way those luscious cones came to perfect peaks capped with cherry tips, but he was also fascinated with the way they sprang back into shape when he released them.

Every time he tried to flatten them or tweaked her nipples hard, Amanda groaned in pleasure just a little louder than before.

He left her breasts and moved his hands down her belly to the tangled patch of pale blonde fleece between her legs. He felt his pole moving in and out, but he sought a different spot, one that would ignite Amanda's passions in a rush. At the top of her delicately sculptured nether lips he found a tiny spire of flesh waiting to be stroked. He pressed his finger into the juicy little button and chased it about as it tried to squirt away under his touch. Every time he pressed down, Amanda's hips went wild.

She surged up and almost flopped on top of him. He kept up the steady stroking in and out of her molten center, but it was the touch between her legs that released her full passion.

"More, Skye, give it all to me. I love you inside me." Amanda bucked up and moved her hips in small quick circles now. His strong arms held her in place so he would not slip out. They moved faster and faster together, somewhat restricted by their position on the bed, but no less aroused because of it.

She ground her hips back into his body. Fargo gave every bit as much pleasure as he got by driving forward and burying himself deep inside her clinging tunnel of female flesh. Stroking over the trembling nether lips and the tiny button at the vertex sent shock waves throughout her tender young body. Amanda shook and groaned and thrashed about beside him until he knew she was getting close to total release.

"Oh, yes, Skye, yeeees!" she cried. Her body snapped back into his groin, taking him as deep inside her as her body would allow.

Fargo held on as if a powerful tornado was trying to blow him away. He kept stroking as she bucked and pitched around on the bed. Then Fargo realized he was losing control. The warmth of her body, the heat of her core, the feel of her striving body, it all pushed him closer to the brink.

He got his arm around her slender waist and pulled her into the circle of his groin. A new bout of sexual release coursed strongly through the woman's body, and this set off the potent tide building inside Fargo. He tried to hold back, but the white-hot surge spewed forth. Amanda sobbed and cried and thrashed around before finally settling down as the fierce winds of desire died down to a gentle breeze.

She spun in Fargo's arms and rested her head on his chest.

"You do so much for me, Skye. You've saved me from

84

being killed so many times. I wish there was more I could do for you."

"More?" He laughed. "If you did any more for me, you'd have to bury me with a smile on my face."

"Wouldn't want to bury you," Amanda said. Then she looked up, her gray eyes twinkling with merriment. "Unless you were really stiff. Then I might join you in the coffin!"

She stroked down his chest and over his limp organ. To neither of their surprises, she coaxed him erect again.

Sunlight angled through the partially opened curtains and warmed the room. Fargo lay on his back, Amanda sleeping peacefully with her head on his shoulder. He held her and felt at peace with the world—for a few seconds—until his mind kicked back into high gear.

Who had sent the two men to kill Amanda the night before? Fargo was sure he had never seen them before and he doubted Amanda had either. They were typical of the roughnecks along the embarcadero who would slit a man's throat for a dollar— or throw a bound woman into San Francisco Bay to drown.

Tracking them down would accomplish nothing. Fargo had wounded one and put a scare into the other. That was about all the punishment they were likely to get, unless they weren't going to collect their blood money until after Amanda was dead. In that case, they had been shot up and run off for nothing.

But they did not look like the thugs frequenting Larson's Lair who called themselves Sydney Ducks. Fargo had the feeling that more than a pair of Ducks would have joined in to kill Amanda, if they had been responsible. While Clay Nance might get someone else do his dirty work for him, it didn't seem likely in Amanda's case. Nance would want McGuire to know who was responsible for killing his star attraction, to keep him and others in line.

McGuire might have other creditors or enemies that Fargo did not know about who would consider permanently removing his star, but his gut feeling told him that was wrong. He had to talk to the theater owner, but knew right now it wouldn't give him anything to go on.

"Where are you going?" Amanda asked in a sleepy voice.

She flopped on the bed and kicked off the sheets and bed-spread to show her complete nakedness. "You aren't going to leave me, are you, Skye?"

"I wanted to get some breakfast."

"Eat here," she said. "I have the best room service you're ever going to find."

"Food," Fargo said.

"Later," the sultry actress said, reaching out her arms to him. As hungry as he was and as anxious as he was to question McGuire, he had to admit, Amanda was right.

11

"I do so want to see what San Francisco has to offer. It is so different from New York and London," Amanda said, craning her neck around to peer past the ledge of the carriage. "When can you take me shopping?"

"I don't know what there is to buy here," Fargo said.

"I have certainly taken note of your paucity of clothing," Amanda said, smiling. In a voice too low for the cabdriver to hear, she added, "I like you with nothing on at all."

"You look mighty fine that way, too," Fargo said. He eyed her up and down as she practically spilled out the bodice of a dress that was too tight for words. In another city she might have been run out of town on a rail for indecency. Here, she attracted attention but no outrage.

That attention was enough to bother Fargo because he still had not decided who was responsible for hiring the two longshoremen to kill her the night before. Amanda had put the kidnapping behind her and was oblivious to the world around her again. But the more she ignored, the more Fargo had to see that she remained unharmed.

"Just one shop," Amanda begged. "I wonder what the fashions look like in San Francisco." The wistfulness of her appeal forced Fargo to relent. He tapped the driver on the shoulder and instructed him what to do. The carriage veered across the street, made a sharp right, and rolled into a section of town Fargo had not yet explored.

Stores along Kearney Street boasted plate-glass windows with goods of all kinds on display.

"I'll stop the driver when you see something that interests you," Fargo said.

"Oh, Skye, you simply do not understand women. I can't shop while we drive past at such speed. I must walk from store to store and see if anything catches my fancy. This will not do." She sat with her hands folded primly in her lap, looking at—through—Fargo.

"Let us out here," he said to the driver. "Wait for us. We'll be back in a half hour."

"A half hour!" cried Amanda. "That's hardly time to look, much less try on any of the fine fashions I see."

"You're due at the theater," Fargo reminded her.

"Yes, of course, we must always feed the idylls of the king," she said with a trace of disdain. "I do so hate it when business interferes with my pleasure. But we have the entire day. A half hour, indeed," Amanda sniffed.

Fargo walked a little behind the actress as she drifted from one window to another, occasionally entering a small shop, but buying nothing. In the end, Amanda purchased a floppy-brimmed hat decorated with flowers. She seemed pleased with it, but Fargo could not see how it was an improvement over her other, smaller hat.

"Do you like it, Skye?" she asked, turning her head from side to side.

"It hides your face," he said.

"That doesn't matter," Amanda said, although she was pleased with his sideways compliment. "It's fashionable. Do you see many women wearing them in the streets?"

Fargo looked around and saw a few other women wearing the huge hats. "Why wear something everyone else wears?"

"You wear those buckskins. Don't all frontiersmen wear them?"

"Not all," he said. "I shot the deer myself, cleaned and tanned the hide. The buckskins are tough and—"

"And functional, yes, I know," she said, wrinkling her nose. "I prefer something dainty and ever so chic."

"Do you have rehearsals today?" he asked, going back to the only excuse he could think of that might move her. Fargo wanted some time away from both the theater and guarding Amanda, so he could track down Clay Nance and settle matters once and for all. The Sydney Ducks' leader was probably harder to find in the day, but once found, dealing with him might be easier. Fargo figured most of the gang operated after sundown, and he might stand a chance to take on Nance one-on-one while the other Ducks slept.

"No, we don't rehearse once a play starts. There is no need if it is going well. And *Easy Lynne* is going marvelously well, thank you. You sound as if you are trying to abandon me," Amanda said peevishly.

"I want to protect you, but it's getting harder. Did the men last night give you any hint who had hired them?"

"Hired them? I thought they took me to the docks to sell me to some horrible captain plying the waves to the Celestial Kingdom. Why, a lovely blonde woman such as I would fetch a handsome price in the Orient. What Chinese emperor wouldn't want me for his harem?"

"None," Fargo said, not wanting to enlighten her as to what had really happened the prior night. Those men had not intended to sell her to a seafaring captain, no matter what romantic fantasy she might have conjured in her head. They went directly to the pier, where they had stashed anchor chain, with the intent of dumping her in the bay. They had been hired to kill her, not sell her into slavery.

"There, that's settled," Amanda said. "Now, let's drive around in this wonderful sunlight, enjoy the fine weather and not think of a single bad thing the rest of the day. Then you can see that I get to the theater in time for the six o'clock performance."

She chattered happily about this and that the remainder of the day. It was with some relief when Fargo finally noted that it was time to head for the Montgomery Street Melodeon.

If anything, Amanda rambled on even more as the carriage drove them to the theater. Fargo listened with half an ear, his real concern being the people along the street. He did not expect any of them to jump up and try to shoot Amanda, but he was becoming suspicious of anyone he did not know—and most of those he did know. He spotted a few reporters from the opening night and even returned a wave from Willie Watkins, who tried to push through a knot of people and come to the carriage. Fargo ordered the driver to speed up so they could leave the newsman behind.

"Oh, Skye, that was Willie back there. We should have offered him a ride to the theater. I am sure he wanted to return for another night's performance. He is quite taken with me."

"No time," Fargo lied. He doubted Willie Watkins was a threat, but he wanted to keep Amanda safe, and could do that best by limiting her access to her fans.

"You can be such a mean man when you try," Amanda said, jumping down before he could help her at the back door to the theater. "I'll just have to do something to sweeten you up."

Fargo paid the driver and followed Amanda into the rear of the theater. Most of the cast was onstage, talking prior to the curtain going up. He stared at them and wondered if any of them might have been responsible for the kidnaping and murder attempt. Fargo jumped when Reggie Hall came up behind him.

"Thicker 'n thieves, the lot of 'em," Reggie said. "You and Miss Fredericks were mighty scarce today. Rumors abounded as to how you and her took off."

"Who said that?" Fargo asked.

Reggie shrugged. "Who knows? Desirée was claiming that Miss Fredericks wasn't the trouper she pretended, and had left town for good." Reggie snorted, then spat, accurately hitting a cuspidor at the end of the curtains. "She even got herself all duded up in the costume Miss Fredericks wears."

"Did she?" Fargo said, eyeing Desirée Lefanu more closely. The dark-haired woman was radiant. She laughed and joked and darted about the stage as if everything in her world was perfect. Fargo contrasted that to how dejected she had been before, when Amanda had taken her starring role away.

"She's the understudy, as well as having a couple of other roles in the play, but changing her costume in time to deliver her first line is going to be a chore," Reggie said.

"Maybe she doesn't think she will have to change. An understudy takes over if the star can't appear?"

"That's what they do, but I seen you and Miss Fredericks come in. There's no reason for Desirée to think she's going on as the lead tonight." Reggie cocked his head to one side and peered at Fargo. "Is there?"

"There might be," Fargo said. He stepped back as the cast came off stage, preparing themselves for the curtain. The orchestra fired up a ditty to keep the audience occupied until everyone was set backstage.

Desirée looked at Fargo and gave him a smile that chilled him to the bone. She patted her hair into place and took the spot where Amanda would enter. Fargo started to ask her what she intended to do when Amanda rushed out of her dressing room.

"Make way, make way," the blonde actress said, shooing people away as she hurried to hit her mark. "We don't want to make a paying customer wait for our show, do we?"

Fargo had seen shock and amazement on a woman's face before, but nothing like the expression on Desirée's. She stumbled back a pace and caught herself on the curtains as Amanda pushed her out of the way. Desirée started to say something, but words failed her. The orchestra struck up the opening tune, Amanda bounced her boobs one last time to make sure she was settled in her costume, then whirled on-stage to begin the play.

"You didn't expect to see her tonight, did you?" Fargo asked Desirée.

"What do you mean by that?" Desirée looked daggers at him and then at Amanda as she started her first repartee with the male lead. "She's the star. Why shouldn't she be here on the second night?"

"Because you hired two men to kill her last night," Fargo said. Desirée did not have to confess for Fargo to know she was guilty as sin. Her face went pale as she put her hand over her mouth.

"You can't prove that," she said.

"I don't have to. You did it. I shot one of the men. Is he all right?"

"He was only wo—" Desirée realized she was digging her own grave by confessing any knowledge at all about the incident. "So what if I tried to regain my place as star?" she said angrily. "She can't just come in here and expect to be the headliner."

Fargo started to reply, but heard something unusual above in the catwalk. He looked up to where he had entered the theater and saw a man moving along the flimsy walkway.

"Reggie," Fargo said. "Who's supposed to be above the stage right now?"

"Nobody. All lighting is taken care of below the stage. The footlights are it. We haven't used the spotlight on the catwalk for some time since it broke." Reggie peered up. "Dammit! He's up to no good if someone's there."

"It might be a fan who wants a better view," Fargo said, but he knew in his gut that wasn't right. Something about the furtive way the man moved told him this was a threat rather than a compliment to Amanda's acting.

"Fargo! Look!" Reggie shouted at the same instant Fargo saw the bright flare of a lucifer. The flame touched a piece of rope and lit it like a fuse. It began burning down to where it would ignite the curtains.

"Get everyone out of the theater," Fargo said. "I'll try to put it out."

"No, Fargo, you can't. This place is a tinderbox. It'll go up like a dry pinecone!"

Fargo was already clambering up the rickety ladder leading to the catwalk. The vibration of his boots on the rungs alerted the firebug. The arsonist drew a six-shooter and fired several times at Fargo, driving him back. Then the man made his way along the walkway to the trapdoor Fargo had used to enter the theater before.

"The curtains!" shrieked a woman in the audience.

The crowd reacted like a wounded animal, surging for the few exits and trampling anyone too slow to get out of the way. In the uproar, Fargo heard Horatio McGuire shouting for everyone to remain clam. The theater owner's words fell on deaf ears.

The curtains cascaded down in a fire fall, sending sparks

flying everywhere. Fargo threw up his arm to protect his face, but he saw the heavy cloth collapse on top of Amanda and McGuire. He jumped forward and drew his Arkansas toothpick, daring the rising heat. Two quick slashes cut through the heavy cloth and allowed McGuire to poke out from beneath.

"Crawl," Fargo ordered. "Crawl out of the theater! Don't stand up. The smoke's getting too thick to breathe."

He did not wait to see if McGuire obeyed. Fargo hunted for another lump in the curtain—Amanda Fredericks. She struggled feebly, but could never hope to be free of the burning cloth before the flames devoured her totally. He stabbed and cut and finally created a hole large enough for her to get free.

"Skye!" she gasped.

He shoved her to the floor.

"Smoke's getting heavier. Crawl on your hands and knees. I'll be right behind you."

"Don't know which way is out," she coughed.

"Go straight ahead," Fargo said, since this was away from the smoldering curtain. "You can get out that way." He had to push her along, but they eventually reached the back door and the cool breeze blowing through it from outside.

"Come on, Skye, we made it!" Amanda caught his hand and tugged him down the steps leading to the alley where many of the cast had already gathered.

Fargo saw Reggie and McGuire, in addition to the others who had been onstage. He scanned the crowd, then turned and listened hard, hearing a faint cry for help.

"Desirée," he called. "Where's Desirée?" The cast looked around, but from their befuddled expressions Fargo knew they had no idea where she was. It didn't matter who was in the burning theater crying for help. Fargo had to go.

He jerked free of Amanda's grip and plunged into the fire. The heat struck him like a hammer's blow, driving him to his knees. The smoke was not as thick along the floor, but the temperature seemed to escalate second by second. Fargo wiggled along like a snake on its belly. The curtains had all fallen now and burned with foot-long flames and thick clouds of smoke.

"Help me," came the cry again, weaker and in the direction of the dressing rooms. Fargo grabbed a section of the set and pushed it ahead of him like a plow. It not only protected him from the heat, it also pushed aside the burning coals and hot ash strewn all over the theater floorboards. He reached Amanda's dressing room and looked inside the smoke-filled room.

"Where are you?" he shouted.

"Here," came the still weaker cry from farther along the corridor. Fargo made his way past three progressively smaller dressing rooms until he came to the last one along the corridor. Desirée Lefanu lay on the floor of the tiny room, her legs burned.

"I can't walk," she said. "Rope from the curtains. On fire. I got tangled. It burned!"

Fargo wasted no time listening to her explanation of what had happened. What mattered now was not how she had come to be burned, but how to get her out of the burning building. Fargo grabbed the front of her costume and pulled, but the cloth gave way, leaving him with a handful of torn fabric. He knew the entire building might go up in flames at any instant, trapping them both.

Grabbing another costume from a nearby rack, he looped the skirt around Desirée so it went under her arms. Fargo tied the other end and slid his neck through it so he could pull her like a beast of burden plowing a field.

"I can't move," she sobbed. "It hurts so! Don't leave me!"

Fargo got on all fours and dug in hard. The toes of his boots slipped, but he kept going, driving harder until he felt the woman begin to slide along the floor behind him. From there to the exit, it was a matter of sheer determination and grit. Fargo refused to stop, even to catch his breath. A pause might spell their deaths—and he was not going to leave her behind.

When they burst through the door and tumbled down the

steps to the alley, McGuire and Reggie ran forward to help them away.

"Get a bucket brigade started," Fargo ordered. "The curtains are smoldering. There's a hell of a lot of smoke, but so far it hasn't set fire to the stage or the walls."

In the distance Fargo head the clanging of a fire alarm. The worst threat to any city, especially one as populated as San Francisco, was fire. The wood buildings went up like kindling, spreading to the next and the next. He had seen entire mining towns leveled by raging flames in the span of a few minutes.

"The volunteers are here," McGuire said. "What should they do, Fargo?"

Fargo saw men in leather helmets and red flannel shirts jumping off a large wagon with hand pumps mounted on it. Closer to the bay, they could have dropped a hose into the water and pumped directly onto the fire. Unfortunately they were a half mile away from the docks.

"Get a bucket brigade going," Fargo said. "I was just inside. The curtains are on fire but it hasn't spread to anything else yet."

"You know where to put the water?" asked a man with a shining gold shield on his chest, marking him as the fire captain. "Show us!"

Fargo did. With the dozen volunteer firemen heaving buckets of water from the barrels they carried, Fargo directed them to the fiery curtains sending up huge billows of greasy black smoke. As the fire was put out, steam joined the smoke in discoloring the theater walls.

"That does it," Fargo said, seeing the ruined curtains stretched across the stage. They had been completely drenched by the vigorous application of water.

"Not yet," the fire captain said. "I've seen fires like this pop back to life in a few minutes, as soon as we turned our backs on them. We have to be certain there's not a single coal glowin' anywhere in this place."

The firemen began working methodically throughout the theater, going from the stage to the orchestra pit and then to the seats. More than one fireman found cushions and hot spots on the wood walls that threatened to burst into flames. Only after he had made as second inspection tour to satisfy himself that his men had done their work well did the fire captain accept McGuire's offer of a free dinner for his crew, and all the beer they could drink.

12

"It's nothing short of a miracle," Horatio McGuire said, wiping his florid face with a tattered rag. In doing so he smeared soot that had deposited on his forehead during the fire and gone unnoticed. "I have looked over the theater and can get it open in a day or two. For all the flames, there was not much damage done."

"What of the smell inside?" asked Amanda. "I cannot be expected to deliver my lines if I'm sucking in huge drafts of smoky air. It would be so embarrassing and unprofessional to start coughing—or smudge my makeup with soot." She wrinkled her nose as she stared at the theater owner's filthy face. The soot had discolored his skin and then had begun to run in dirty rivers as the man sweated profusely.

"That won't be a problem," McGuire assured her. "We will air it out in nothing flat. Paint! Whitewash! We can take care of the walls right away. The problem will be curtains, but that is minor. An active seamstress or two can have them back before you know it. I assure you, we shall be onstage and giving the finest performances of the season in only days!" McGuire struck a pose, as if he were John Frémont pointing Lajeunesse, Preuss, and the others to the top of Snow Peak to plant the American flag and find the "solitary pioneer" bumblebee on the continent's tallest mountain.

"What do you think?" Fargo asked the fire captain. The volunteer fireman looked at him in surprise.

"You're asking my opinion about the building?"

"You've seen more fires than any of them," Fargo said, looking directly McGuire.

"He's right," the fireman finally said when he realized Fargo was not pulling his leg. "The walls are still intact. But the lady's right about not being able to breathe good air inside for a long time. No way of airing it out, no matter what the owner says. The smoke clings and makes it hard not to cough." The fire captain hitched up his canvas pants and stared at Amanda. "Wouldn't matter if she was coughing her lungs out," he said. "I'd come see her perform. She's 'bout the purtiest actress in San Francisco."

"Might be you could get some money out of Mr. McGuire if you helped paint the theater and get it ready to open again," Fargo suggested. "He might even give you a few tickets to see Miss Fredericks."

"That's a right good idea," the fireman said, grinning ear to ear. "I got a whole team of men who sit around on their butts doin' nothing most of the day. Volunteer is just another name for idler. Why shouldn't we pick up some extra money? We know more 'bout fires and fixin' stuff than anybody else. Ever try to keep one of those pumper engines working?"

Fargo let the fire captain approach McGuire with the proposal. Considering that the Sydney Ducks had set the fire—Fargo was sure of it—hiring men to repair the theater could be a problem. But the firemen were perfect for the work: already on the scene and tough enough not to be intimidated. Any man who could walk into a blazing building to throw a tiny bucket of water at a fire wasn't likely to blink an eye at a threat by a Duck.

Fargo went to where Desirée huddled on the curb, her arms wrapped around herself as if she were freezing to death. He stared at her until she looked up, a defiant look on her face.

"The two longshoremen," Fargo said.

"What of them?"

"You hired them to kill Amanda."

Desirée shrugged and looked away. "So what? This is a tough business. If she can't protect herself enough to keep her role, she shouldn't be on the stage."

"It's one thing to be a better actress. It's something else to resort to murder to get a role."

"You saved me from the fire," Desirée said unexpectedly. "Why did you do that? You know I hired those men to kill Amanda. You could have let me burn."

"No, I couldn't," Fargo said.

"I suppose not," Desirée said. "What are you going to do now?"

"I can't prove you tried to kill Amanda unless I find the two longshoremen you hired."

"They're long gone. They left San Francisco right after they told me you had chased them off, but they lied to me. They said they had killed the bitch!"

"You ought to join them," Fargo said.

"I don't know where they went." Desirée was sullen.

"Hunt for them. Anywhere but San Francisco. Now." Fargo put a steely edge in his command.

"You're running me out of town? You saved my life to tell me to beat it?"

"You have one hour," Fargo said. "After that you'll be living on borrowed time."

"She means that much to you? That peroxide-blonde bitch? She's not even a good actress!"

"One hour," Fargo repeated. Desirée Lefanu grumbled, got to her feet, and stumbled off, glaring at him over her shoulder once before rounding the corner and vanishing. Fargo hoped this was the last he would see of her. He didn't hold with paid killers, but he really despised men—or women—who wouldn't do their own dirty work.

Fargo went to where McGuire was finishing his agreement with the volunteer firemen to begin repairs on the theater.

"A splendid stroke of luck that the fire captain wanted to help repair the theater. It might have taken days to get a crew together, otherwise." McGuire rubbed his hands together, not realizing Fargo's part in getting the volunteers onto the job.

"What can you do about the arsonist?" asked Fargo. "I didn't get a good look at his face, but he must have been a Sydney Duck."

"I don't doubt that he was," McGuire said, his good humor fading. "With the cost of repair, how can I possibly pay their extortion money and keep operating?"

"What can the city police do for you?" Fargo hesitated mentioning the Specials. His run-in with the Specials working for Clay Nance had convinced him they were nothing more than hired killers.

"Not much. I wish the federal marshal had a stronger presence in town, but he does not. The marshal lets the local police do the work while he spends his time across the bay. I could hire a squad of Specials," McGuire said, chewing on his lower lip. Before Fargo could tell him what a mistake that would be, McGuire shook his head. "No, I dare not do that. I don't have the money to pay the Sydney Ducks. How could I hope to get enough to pay the Specials? They are an avaricious bunch."

"What can you do to protect your theater?" Fargo asked. "The Ducks will keep up their attacks if you don't do something."

"Politics," McGuire said, brightening again. "I know this sounds odd, but if the politicians who run the city are on my side, the Ducks might not try to extort money from me."

"It's not extortion if they're asking for repayment of a loan," Fargo said. "Could you get a bank to loan you the money so you could pay off the Sydney Ducks?"

"They are insatiable," McGuire said. "But you might have an idea there, Fargo. If I can make contacts with enough of the city fathers, I might get one to co-sign on a loan at a bank."

"That doubles your protection," Fargo said. "What politician would want to lose money because the Ducks are threatening to burn you out?"

"Yes, a political alliance. I like it. A wonderful idea!" McGuire looked around, then waved at a well-dressed man on the far side of the street. "Mayor Van Ness! How nice of you to come by."

McGuire hurried to speak with San Francisco's mayor. Fargo saw several other prosperous looking men gravitate over when McGuire began making his extravagant promises. If anyone could win over the San Francisco politicians, it was the theater owner.

Fargo ignored Amanda waving to him as he went up the steps into the backstage area. He turned and looked at the crowd of gawkers, hunting for anyone who might belong to the Sydney Ducks. They had to know by now that their arson attempt had failed and that McGuire would be open again in a few days. That meant Nance would order a second attempt.

Or would he? Fargo didn't know how the gang leader's mind worked. The attempt to burn the melodeon to the ground might have been effective no matter what happened. Lose the theater, get even with Horatio McGuire for not repaying his loan and giving into extortion. Have it remain standing, and the arson acted as a goad to the owner to pony up the money Nance demanded.

Fargo worried less about the theater than he did about Amanda's safety. She was in good hands at the moment with Reggie Hall at her side. He stood with his thumbs hooked into his suspenders, both six-shooters openly displayed where he had them stuck into his belt. Fargo studied the men around them but saw no one who didn't seem to belong to the area.

He went into the theater and looked up at the proscenium arch. It appeared intact. The fire captain had not lied when he said the theater would be as good as new with some paint and a few repairs here and there. Fargo stared up at the catwalk where the arsonist had set the curtains on fire and wondered if he might find any trace of the man.

Tracking through a city was almost impossible, even for the Trailsman, but Fargo felt he had to do something. Standing around waiting for the Sydney Ducks to strike again made him uneasy. Better to seek out Nance, and put an end to the trouble, than to wait apprehensively for Amanda or someone else to be harmed.

Fargo's hand went to the butt of his six-shooter when he heard movement above his head, along the catwalk where the arsonist had been. He saw a dim figure moving furtively. Fargo drew his six-gun, sighted along the barrel, then lowered his pistol. It was a difficult shot at best—and he didn't want the man dead.

Taking the rungs two at a time, he scrambled up the ladder to the catwalk and stepped out on it. The flimsy structure swayed under his weight, making him worry that the fire had damaged some of the ropes supporting it. One wrong step and he might find himself plunging three stories to the stage below.

And it might not even take a misstep. The entire structure might simply collapse.

Fargo sidled along the catwalk. He saw the open trapdoor leading to the roof and caught a hint of sea air through it. His lungs had been burning from the smoky smell permeating the theater, and this fresh air revived him and his spirits. Fargo walked faster and got to the edge of the trapdoor. He warily poked his head up and chanced a quick look around.

There was no one in sight.

Fargo pulled himself up and looked around the up-and-down peaks of the theater roof. Canting his head to one side, he listened hard. Through the usual sounds of the city and harbor beyond he heard a scraping noise as someone walked over the roof.

He made his say to the peak and looked at the slope beyond, expecting to see Nance or another of his henchmen.

"Watkins!" he called.

The reporter for the *San Francisco Herald* turned at hearing his name and lost his balance. He threw his hands into the air and slid backward, his feet slipping as if they were on ice. With a shriek, he fell over the edge of the roof.

Fargo wasted no time vaulting over the peak and sliding down the shingled roof to the edge. He adroitly caught himself at the edge of the roof and looked over to see the reporter dangling from the gutter.

"Mr. Fargo, please! Help!" Willie Watkins called.

Fargo flopped onto his belly and thrust out his hand for the newsman to take. For a moment, Fargo thought they would both go tumbling over the side to land in the street beside the theater. Then he kicked off a shingle, got a toehold in the wood beam underneath, and found enough leverage to heave the reporter up beside him.

"Thanks, Mr. Fargo. You saved my bacon, that's for sure."

"What are you doing up here?" Fargo asked, sitting up. The slick wood shingles made any movement dangerous.

"I wanted a story. I'm not doing anything but society reporting and figured to get a real bang-up exclusive that would make my editor assign me to the city desk."

"That doesn't tell me why you're on the theater roof."

Fargo began moving back up the roof. Watkins hastily followed him to the trapdoor on the other side of the peak in the roof. Seated on the edge of the trapdoor they faced each other, their legs dangling down.

"This wasn't an accident," Watkins said almost conspiratorially. "I want to prove that the Sydney Ducks are behind it."

"How'd you come to that conclusion?" Fargo saw the way the reporter flushed and averted his eyes guiltily. For a brief second, Fargo wondered if Watkins might not be in cahoots with Nance. Then the truth came out.

"I sort of overheard it. One of the crime reporters got a tip that the Ducks were going to torch the place. He didn't care, so I followed up on it, but I got here too late."

"The fire was already out?" Fargo had to laugh. That wasn't too late. That was the best time to come by. The danger posed by the combustible theater was so great that nowhere in the city would have been safe if it had gone up the way the Ducks had intended.

"Go on, make fun of me," Watkins said harshly. "I'm going to be a great reporter some day. This is the kind of story that gets you noticed."

"Why did you come up on the catwalk?"

"I saw the way the flames had burned the stage curtains and decided the fire must have started up here. If I could find something incriminating, I could follow the lead and get my scoop."

Fargo studied the young reporter closely. Nance and his gang were tougher than the young reporter imagined, and they would just as soon dump his lifeless body in the bay for the sharks as they would knock back a shot of whiskey. In other words, for pleasure. Getting the goods on the Sydney Ducks must have been tried before—and the Ducks still ruled San Francisco.

"It's not much of a story that the Sydney Ducks are involved in arson and other crimes, is it?" asked Fargo.

"Well, no, but so far no one's gotten a complete story telling how far their influence extends through the city. How many other theaters are they shaking down?"

"They're dangerous men," Fargo said. He saw the way

103

Watkins's jaw firmed and caught the look of a crusader in his eyes.

"All the more reason to bring them to justice."

"So you publish a few stories and get San Francisco up in arms?" asked Fargo.

"I can do it. You haven't been here all that long, Mr. Fargo. You don't know about the Vigilance Committees of a few years ago and what happened when James King of William was killed. Charles Cora killed him right in the *Bulletin* office and then hightailed it out of town. Billy Mulligan was the sheriff and a friend of Cora's. Well, the Second Vigilance Committee formed and took care of matters."

"They hanged Cora?" Fargo had heard similar stories throughout the West.

"That was what happened, yes, sir," Watkins said with some satisfaction. "Some wanted to hang Sheriff Mulligan, too, but they were law-abiding citizens and disbanded."

"You said this was the Second Vigilance Committee. Does San Francisco form a vigilante group every time the lawmen get too corrupt?" The notion struck Fargo as absurd. If the sheriffs and marshals didn't do their duty, replace them. Perhaps put them in jail, but definitely get rid of them.

"San Francisco has always had trouble policing itself. That's why there are Specials everywhere. They're sort of a private police force that patrols where the regular coppers won't go."

"I know," Fargo said dryly. Watkins looked at him strangely, but said nothing. "I saw the man who set the fire, but I didn't get a good enough look to identify him. I intend to stop Nance from trying to harm Amanda Fredericks or burn down Horatio McGuire's theater."

"Nance? Is he the leader of the Sydney Ducks?" Watkins fumbled in his pocket for a notebook. Fargo saw he was giving the young reporter information he had not known.

"You can get killed crossing these men," Fargo said.

"I don't care. If I want to be a real reporter, not one telling about garden parties and afternoon teas, I have to take risks."

Fargo had seen no way of bringing Clay Nance to justice before, but he did now. With Willie Watkins reporting on the criminal tendrils of the Sydney Ducks that spread throughout the city, enough citizens might become incensed enough to do something about it. Fargo did not like the idea of a vigilante committee, but it was sometimes the only way justice was achieved.

"We might team up to go after the Sydney Ducks," Fargo said.

Willie Watkins's eyes widened in surprise, then he thrust out his hand as if he thought Fargo would change is mind.

"Shake on it—partner!" he cried.

Fargo took the young man's hand and shook, wondering what the hell he was letting himself in for.

13

"It will be a triumph of the theater," Amanda said grandly. "Imagine. A complimentary performance for all the most powerful politicians in the city."

"Imagine a politician getting anything for free," Fargo said sardonically. "I don't now why McGuire wanted to do this before the melodeon is repainted."

"To show those horrible Sydney Ducks we have no fear of them, of course," Amanda said. "We will put on the show for those most likely to tun their might against the evil boiling out of Sydney-Town. McGuire told me James Van Ness is not only mayor of this wonderful town but also recorder. That's a police judge. With him on our side, how can we not prevail?" Amanda made another grand gesture, swirled her skirts, and struck another pose. Fargo saw she was speaking less than she was acting. The actress lived on drama, and this performance on a bare stage, amid singed walls, gave her a full dose.

"She'll be safe enough during the performance," Reggie Hall said confidently, hands on the six-shooters shoved into his belt. The old man looked as if he could whip his weight in wildcats. He had come alive after the fire and had more than once said he wanted to settle accounts with the Ducks.

"I've got to find Nance and get this straight," Fargo said. If he and Nance could talk, Fargo was sure the leader of the Sydney Ducks would settle for the money McGuire owed him on his loan and stop trying to extort extra money.

"How will you convince him?" asked Reggie. "He wants to make an example out of McGuire."

"If he finds he's cutting off his nose to spite his face, he'll back off. He wants the money McGuire owes him, not a tornado spinning through his small empire causing more trouble than he can imagine."

"You're going to be the tornado?" Reggie chuckled. "Well, son, I reckon you're the one who can do it."

"Skye, oh, Skye!" called Amanda, hurrying over to him. "I don't know what happened. I was just talking to the director and he said Desirée hasn't been seen since the fire."

"What a shame," Fargo said, trying to keep his voice neutral.

"Several others are missing, too. I need at least two extras. You won't need to change into a costume since we won't have sets or curtains up." Amanda pursed her lips, then began pointing to the spot where she wanted Fargo. He considered walking onto the stage again with an audience watching his every move, even if this was more a rehearsal than a real play.

"I'm sorry, Amanda," he told her. "I have business. Important business."

"Nothing is as important as the play," she said, astounded at his reluctance to go on stage again.

"The show must go on," Reggie cut in, "but Miss Fredericks, Mr. Fargo's working on a real big money problem for McGuire. The theater might not get the paint it needs, 'less he tracks down a backer." Reggie winked broadly in Fargo's direction. The lie was appreciated because it saved Fargo from having to convince her his business was more important than hers.

"Oh, bother," Amanda said, stamping her foot in pique. She frowned and then walked off muttering to herself, "Money, always money. 'Money is like muck, not good except it be spread.' "

Fargo turned to go and ran into Willie Watkins. The reporter stared up at him, looking expectant.

"Mr. Fargo, you said I could go along when you went to Sydney-Town. That's where you're heading, isn't it?"

"Don't you have to cover the performance for your paper?" Fargo asked.

"I'm supposed to, but this is more important. To me, Mr. Fargo. When we were on the roof, you promised. I know it's dangerous. I don't care because this is something I have to do or forever damn myself as a coward."

Fargo glanced at Reggie, who was trying not to laugh. He shook his head, as if saying, "I squared you with Amanda. You have to handle Watkins on your own."

"Come on," Fargo said, against his better judgment.

"With you all the way, Mr. Fargo!"

"Tell me about Sydney-Town," Fargo asked Watkins.

The reporter fiddled with his pencil and finally tucked his notebook into a coat pocket, when he realized there was nothing to take note of at the moment. They stood at a corner a few blocks away from Larson's Lair, surrounded by a rougher element than near the Montgomery Street Melodeon.

"It was settled by convicts from Australia," Watkins said.

"I don't want history, I want something that will help cut Nance from the herd of desperadoes."

Willie Watkins looked like he had just been told his ship was sinking under him.

"I don't know that much about Nance," Watkins admitted. "What I overheard was—"

"Worthless," Fargo said in disgust. He was sorry he had brought the reporter with him now. It was hard enough to watch his own back without having to wet-nurse a man completely out of his element.

"Maybe not, Mr. Fargo," Watkins said, struggling to make himself useful. "I'm expert at asking questions and getting information. Let me try to flush him."

"I don't want to flush him like a bird, I want to—" Fargo pushed Watkins back, then grabbed his arm and pulled him into an alley where they could kneel down behind a pile of garbage. "Specials," Fargo hissed.

Four of the blue-coated private policemen strolled along, laughing and using their clubs to bang on doors and poke one another roguishly. They passed within a yard of Fargo without seeing him.

"Are you afraid of them?" whispered Watkins, poking his head out and looking around the edge of the building to watch the retreating Specials.

"No," Fargo said flatly. "But I know better than to get into a fight that will keep me from finding Nance." He hurried down the street going away from the Specials, but Fargo knew the private policemen patrolled every inch of Sydney-Town. There was no doubt they were all on the take from Nance, no matter who their avowed employers might be.

"The businesses here don't see many regular coppers, because they stay down around City Hall," Watkins said. "The Specials aren't so bad, are they? Have you had a run-in with them?"

"Ask your questions to find Nance," Fargo said. He stopped at the intersection a block from Larson's Lair. Two Sydney Ducks stood guard outside, clubs resting beside them on the wood-planked street as they sat on a broken curb. One held his head as if he had a monumental headache and the other stared drunkenly into the distance. Fargo estimated his chances of walking past the pair and decided they were not good.

"Go ply your trade on those two," Fargo said. "If they get rough, you leave right away. I'll meet you back in the alley where we hid from the Specials."

"Behind the garbage," Watkins said, wiping his nose as he remembered the fetid odor. "What do you intend doing, Mr. Fargo?"

Fargo did not answer. He pushed Watkins toward the men and waited to see their reaction. Willie Watkins spoke for almost a minute before he got a rise out of them. Then it was everything Fargo could have hoped for. The men were still drunk from their night's debauchery and intended to have sport with Watkins.

The young reporter lit out like a jackrabbit, the two Sydney Ducks stumbling after him. Fargo had no doubt that Watkins could easily outleg them in their condition. He walked boldly to the door of Larson's Lair, looked up and down the street to be sure he was unseen, then went inside.

The dim interior forced him to pause a few seconds so his eyes could adapt. When they did, Fargo saw men sprawled over tables and on the floor. The bartender lay on the bar, snoring loudly. Fargo walked to the rear of the saloon, hunting for Clay Nance. He grabbed a handful of hair on the head of a man lying facedown on a poker table where Nance had been gambling, and lifted.

The man's eyes fluttered open, then he yelped.

"Goddamn! It ain't no dream! This's the one I was supposed to kill!"

Fargo slammed the Special's head forward, banging his forehead off the table. But it was too late. The cry roused others in the saloon. It had been his bad luck to awaken the Special Nance had ordered to get rid of him back at their crude calaboose.

Two Sydney Ducks came at him. Fargo sidestepped a clumsy jab and pushed the man backward so hard he fell on the floor in a drunken heap. The second Duck was more sober. He threw a punch, catching Fargo on the cheek and turning his head.

If he stayed to fight, Fargo knew he would have the whole gang on his neck. He danced back, let his foe miss with a looping punch, and then slid a chair into the man's legs. As the man went down, Fargo broke an empty whiskey bottle over his head.

The shrill bleat of a whistle forced him to turn. The Special he had mistaken for Clay Nance sounded the alarm to summon backup.

"Come on, men, come on and grab him! Nance wants him dead."

"Aw, shaddup, Hayworth," growled the barkeep. He tried to roll over on the bar and tumbled to the floor. The drunken man pushed himself up to a sitting position.

"Get him," Hayworth cried. "Nance wants him dead, and I don't have my gun!"

Fargo pushed past the Special and went through the back storeroom and into the alley behind Larson's Lair. Inside the saloon Hayworth kept tooting his whistle to get other Specials on Fargo's trail, but he had little luck drawing any. It might have been too early in the morning. From the condition of the revelers in Larson's Lair, they had been on a real bender the night before. Fargo hoped the Specials had joined it and were now sleeping it off.

"Stop!" Hayworth cried, following Fargo into the alley. Fargo saw Hayworth had picked up a six-shooter. He lifted it and fired. Luckily his aim was as bad as his breath.

Fargo ducked, dodged back onto the street in front of the

saloon, and looked around for Willie Watkins. The reporter was nowhere to be seen, but Hayworth refused to give up in his attempt to kill Fargo. He stumbled along behind, shooting as he came.

Knowing it was only a matter of time before Hayworth attracted the attention of the Specials patrolling Sydney-Town, Fargo took off at a ground-devouring run. He wasn't certain where he was headed, but soon saw how the nature of the buildings changed. Gone were the trappings he recognized. Replacing them were Chinese ideograms and strange items put on the street for sale.

He had returned to Chinatown. Fargo slowed his pace, cut down a narrow debris-strewn alley and emerged on the next street over. Dupont Gai, he had heard this street called. He saw the man he had helped unload the wagon twenty yards off.

"Won Li!" he called. Then Fargo noticed everyone in the street was slowly vanishing like fog in the hot morning sun. Doors closed and locking bars dropped. Windows were shuttered. Even those women peering out from second-story windows disappeared.

He spun and saw the reason for the Celestials making themselves so scarce. Hayworth had found the band of four Specials that Fargo and Watkins had avoided earlier and all five were storming down Dupont Gai toward him.

Fargo knew he could never fight it out with all five men. He had a fully loaded six-shooter but stopping five burly men with six shots was a feat he would have a hard time achieving. He ran like a fool, his boots making sharp pounding sounds on the cobblestoned street as he hunted for a place to hide.

Everything was securely buttoned up because the Chinese had seen the Specials before he had.

"Get him, get him!" shouted Hayworth. "Nance wants him dead. There's a good price on his head, too!"

One Special, fleeter of foot than the others, caught up with Fargo and shoved him hard enough to make him break stride and stumble. Before Fargo could regain his balance, he was tackled to the ground. They went down in a heap, rolling over and over across the littered street. Fargo was stronger and a better wrestler than his opponent and slipped free, spinning around behind the man. Fargo's strong forearm clamped over the Special's windpipe, but he saw he might kill the man and lose everything.

The fight had given Hayworth and his cronies time to catch up.

"You're Fargo. Nance told me," Hayworth said, clutching his six-shooter in his hand as if it might try to run away at any second. From this and other details, Fargo knew Hayworth wasn't too adept with the pistol.

"Is this your first week on the job?" Fargo asked.

"How'd you know?" Hayworth's bloodshot eyes went wide in surprise.

"You want to jaw with him or kill the son of a bitch?" growled another of the Specials. "Lemme pound his head in."

"I'll break this one's neck," Fargo said, tightening his grip on the corded throat under his arm. The man let out trapped animal sounds but could not form words. Fargo preferred it that way.

"Go on," Hayworth said. "Kill him. Nobody cares."

Fargo tried backing up and knew he could not do it as long as he held the man. Shoving his captive into the others, Fargo vaulted over a wagon, rolled to the other side, and hit the ground running. His only hope was to outrun the Specials since he could not hope to outfight them.

Before Fargo got halfway down the block, he slowed and glanced over his shoulder. Where five men had been chasing him, he counted only four now. He stopped running and watched as another Special just . . . vanished. A hook had popped out from the doorway of a store and then jerked back, the Special grasping at the barb embedded in his throat.

Two more Specials were tripped or clubbed by unseen assailants. Hayworth and one other caught up with Fargo.

"Giving up, eh? That's good. Makes it easier to kill you."

"Like you tried before?" taunted Fargo. He played for time. And he was rewarded when a silken noose lowered from the second-story window above them. With a soft swishing sound, the silk noose dropped over the Special's head, tightened around his throat and then pulled him, kicking, upward until he was halfway to the window. Then he hung limply. Fargo

112

didn't have to check to see if the man was dead. The protruding tongue and ugly crimson flush on his face showed that.

Fargo faced Hayworth.

"I might be able to save you," Fargo said.

"What're ya talkin' 'bout?" Hayworth demanded. "We got ya and this time you ain't gettin' away."

" 'We'?"

Hayworth looked left and right, then whirled around. The other four Specials had disappeared as if they had never existed.

"What did ya do to 'em?"

"Drop your six-gun," Fargo said, "and you might get out of Chinatown alive."

"Chinkie town?" Hayworth took a good look around for the first time and turned as pale as a bleached linen sheet. "I didn't know we'd come this far."

"Drop your gun," Fargo said sharply. In the shadows of a recessed doorway he saw a glint of light off a wicked silver hook. From the other side of the street came three Celestials with hatchets, all looking as if they could use them. Their silent approach spooked Hayworth more than the way his friends had vanished.

"It was Nance that wanted you dead. I just joined the Specials. I needed the money. Honest, Fargo! I don't even *like* Nance."

"You've never been honest a day in your life," Fargo said.

"Please, don't let them yellow devils kill me. They're tong killers!"

Hayworth fell to his knees and begged Fargo for mercy. Fargo was still trying to hide his surprise at the ease with which the Chinese had removed his pursuers.

"Mr. Fargo, there you are! You were supposed to wait for me in that alley!" Willie Watkins came running up. Fargo cursed under his breath. He wasn't sure he would get away from the Celestial killers and now he had to worry about the reporter, too.

Watkins stopped and saw the black-pajama-clad men slowly moving in for the kill. He called to them in a singsong that stopped them in their tracks. The tong killers with the hatchets backed off, put their heads together for a second, then strutted away arrogantly.

"I didn't know you spoke their lingo," Fargo said.

"I know some," Watkins said. "I told them we were friends. At least, I think I said that."

"You say you devil who steal souls," said Won Li. "They not want their souls taken."

"Oh," said Willie Watkins, frowning. Then, "Who are you?"

"He's my benefactor. Thank you, Won Li." Fargo imitated the bow he had seen the Chinese use among themselves. Won Li returned it.

"You help. You not like other *mogui*. This one speaks." Won Li laughed and said, "Bad speak, but he try."

"Yes, that's right," Watkins said, his head bobbing like it was on a spring. "I try."

"The Specials?" Fargo asked. He read the verdict in Won Li's eyes. The Specials should not have invaded territory that was not theirs to patrol. They were dead at the hands of the tong.

"We, uh, we should go, Mr. Fargo. It's g-getting late," Watkins said. He tugged at Fargo's sleeve. Fargo had already seen the men with the variety of wicked silver hooks, swords and silk ropes coming from their hiding places.

"Don't let them kill me," pleaded Hayworth.

"I'll do what I can," Fargo said, "but you're mine if I get you out of here. Do you understand?"

"Anything you want, I'll do it. I'm your man. Please!"

"He lies," Won Li said.

"It's going to be hard convincing him not to let his friends kill you," Fargo said to Hayworth. "You intruded where you weren't welcome."

"I'll spy on Nance for you, if that's what you want. I know there's bad blood between you two. I'll kill him for you if you'll let me go!"

"You'd do as good a job as you did on me," Fargo said sarcastically. "But I need someone who can tell me where to find Nance, someone he trusts."

"He—he's gone right now. He went down the coast and won't be back for a day or two. I kin let ya know when he comes home. I can! First thing, when Nance returns, I'll let ya know!"

Fargo knew Hayworth was lying to save his own miserable hide, but the Special might prove useful later. How, Fargo was not sure, but he wasn't too keen on seeing more blood spilled. That gained nothing but ill will on all sides.

"Will you let him leave, Won Li? So he can get back to Sydney-Town alive?"

Won Li bowed deeply. "Our debt is paid," the Celestial said.

"No," Fargo said. "I am deeply in your debt. Should you want help, all you need to do is ask."

Won Li flashed a small smile, then went to Hayworth and yelled, "*Hai!*"

Hayworth shrieked in fear, scrambled along the street on hands and knees until he got his feet under him, and he took off running.

"I hope his heart doesn't explode from fright," Watkins said. Then he sobered when he saw the Chinese with swords and silken strangling cords moving closer.

"Is there anything I can do for you now?" asked Fargo. He looked from Won Li to the tong killers and then back.

"Go," Won Li said. "You hurry. But no need to go as fast as that one!"

Fargo heard laughter ripple through the Celestials. He grabbed Watkins's arm and pulled the young reporter after him, thanking his lucky stars that he was still alive.

14

"I should have told Hayworth how well Mr. McGuire is connected," Willie Watkins said, scribbling in his notebook. "That would have cemented his loyalty."

Fargo tried to keep from laughing at the young man's naïveté. Hayworth might have been afraid of Fargo—and Won Li— but he was even more afraid of Clay Nance and the Sydney Ducks. he would have made any promise to get away alive. In spite of this, Fargo thought he had heard just a hint of slyness in the Special's promise that might mean he would pass along information to Fargo. There seemed to be a power struggle going on between Hayworth and Nance that might prove to his benefit.

What worried Fargo was that the information would come straight from Nance's mouth, with Hayworth hoping Fargo and Nance would kill each other. Fargo did not want to walk into a trap when he finally went to settle accounts with the leader of the Sydney Ducks.

They took the steps up to the stage door two at a time. Fargo rapped on the door and waited until he heard shuffling footsteps inside the theater.

"You boys got back just in time," Reggie said, opening the door for them. The old man hitched up his belt and settled the two six-guns more comfortably. "Miss Fredericks's performance is about over."

"Is it going well?" Watkins asked eagerly. "This will make a fine follow-up story to go with our excursion into Sydney-Town."

Fargo started to tell the reporter not to print anything about trying to stop Nance's extortion. If the Sydney Ducks read about their intentions—and had any cause to doubt Hayworth's loyalty—more than the Montgomery Street Melodeon might go up in flames.

"She's been out there givin' the performance of a lifetime," Reggie said proudly. "I hope them no-good politicians appreciate what they're gettin' for nothing." Reggie hawked up a gob and shot it toward the cuspidor. The loud ringing sound as it hit the brass spittoon was drowned out by the thunderous applause from the audience. Amanda was taking a bow for her fine performance, then beckoned the rest of the cast to join her onstage.

But Fargo knew the audience applauded Amanda, in spite of the lack of costumes, in spite of having the performance in a partly burned-out theater in the middle of the afternoon.

Fargo looked up to the box above the stage where he had spotted Nance before. Dark streaky fingers of soot left by the flames had turned the area into an inky pit. He stared at the darkness until he was certain nothing moved up there. Fargo moved out into the wings so he could look over the audience. The droves of men had jumped to their feet, cheering and applauding loudly.

"They obviously appreciated it," Fargo said. He worried that the politicians and their aides would rush the stage like any other drunken audience, each demanding a private session with Amanda. When two men got to the edge of the stage and started to pull themselves up, Fargo moved to block them.

Horatio McGuire got there before him. McGuire waved Fargo back, knelt, and huffed and puffed as he helped one man up. The other coming from the far side of the stage Fargo recognized as Mayor James Van Ness. He wondered if the politician was in Nance's hip pocket or if there was a power struggle between the men for control of San Francisco. It might have been a case of each with his own sphere of command, Nance running the crime in Sydney-Town and Van Ness everything else.

Fargo would have to ask Watkins how politics in San Francisco worked. From the stories he had heard about vigilantes, the politicians were not always honest or in control. Having both the mayor's power and that of a police judge in one man's hands must sorely tempt Van Ness, too, no matter how honest he might want to be.

"Gentlemen," boomed the mayor, addressing the audience. "It is with great pleasure I pronounce this one hell of a fine performance!" The mayor's words were met with great cheering. The other man escorted by McGuire whispered to the theater owner, pointed into the wings, then whispered some more. Fargo wondered who the man was and why McGuire lavished so much attention on him. He found out quickly.

"Mr. Fargo," McGuire said. "Can you show Mr. Trevor around? He, uh, he's the building inspector for San Francisco. I am sure he would be especially interested in inspecting Miss Fredericks's dressing room."

Fargo bristled. McGuire made it sound as if he considered Amanda nothing more than a cheap whore whose body would be sold to further the fortunes of the theater owner.

"Oh, it's not like that," McGuire said, coming to speak in a low tone to Fargo when he saw his expression. "Mr. Trevor's wife wants to be an opera star, and I told him Amanda would be happy to give some advice. She is an old hand at such meetings, I am sure."

"Yeah," Fargo said sourly. He didn't want any part of this, but saw no way around it. He was not going to walk out and let Amanda face the masses of men alone. Any of them might work for Nance or have other reasons for wanting her dead. For all he knew, Desirée still had friends who wanted Amanda removed from her starring role so the dark-haired actress could take over. He had assumed the role of her protector and was not going to walk away if she might come to harm. All he had to do was put an end to Nance's threats.

"Thank you so much!" cried Amanda, waving to the men in the audience as they left the theater. As the rest of the cast exited the stage, Amanda let the mayor take her arm. They walked slowly, heads close together as they chattered away like old friends.

"Mr. McGuire has some other business to tend to and wanted me to show you around," Fargo said, seeing the theater owner moving among those in the audience, pumping hands and slapping others on the back. The mayor was important, as was the building inspector, but McGuire needed more allies than just the two of them. From the way those he spoke with laughed and passed him their business cards, Fargo figured he was on his way to forging the bonds he needed to stay in business.

"I need to get a crew in to inspect the theater from the roof down to the foundations. Those walls look suspiciously wobbly to me."

"That a building term?" asked Reggie. "I know a lot of gents who get wobbly, do good work and have for a lot of years."

Fargo motioned the old man to silence. It did no good antagonizing someone who might take it into his head to close down the melodeon for personal reasons. Looking around the shell of a theater, Fargo knew there were grounds for shutting the place down because of weakened walls.

Fargo went with Trevor and Willie Watkins through the wings toward the actress's dressing room.

"This old place ought to be razed," Trevor said, looking around. "I'm surprised it didn't fall down on its own before the fire."

"The theater's in decent enough shape," Reggie protested.

"Some things in the theater are in *great* shape," Trevor said, leering at Amanda. Fargo wondered if McGuire was right about the man wanting nothing more than advice on his wife's career from Amanda. Still, he had to agree with Trevor. Seeing Amanda bustling along ahead of them in the narrow corridor, her hindquarters waggling seductively, convinced Fargo that watching after her safety was well worth his while.

"Tell me, Mr. Trevor," said Watkins, "about your job at City Hall. It must be exciting, getting to meet stars like Miss Fredericks."

"Who're you?" Trevor asked.

"A reporter for the *Herald*, sir. I do stories on crime in the city."

"Why are you here?" Trevor asked, stepping back from

Watkins. Fargo saw how uneasy the inspector was, but Watkins plowed on.

"There are undercurrents here, sir, that you would not believe. At least you wouldn't until I get them into print."

"He's quite the crusadin' reporter," chimed in Reggie.

"I see," Trevor said. He looked toward Amanda's dressing room, where the door stood ajar. In the room she joked with the mayor, but it was obvious Van Ness was getting ready to leave. Trevor was caught between pursuing what Fargo believed to be less than honorable intentions with Amanda—with McGuire's tacit surrender to such advances—and being revealed in one of Watkins's stories.

"The building looks stable enough," Trevor said suddenly. "Perhaps I can return later to do a more detailed examination."

"Anytime," Fargo said. "I'm sure Mr. McGuire will be glad to escort you wherever you want. And I have some familiarity with the roof, if you need to investigate there after checking Miss Fredericks's dressing room—after she's left." He put a sharper edge to his words to let Trevor know how dangerous it would be if he crossed McGuire or tried to do anything unseemly with Amanda.

"Mr. Mayor!" Trevor called when Van Ness came out of Amanda's room. "I wanted to let you know there's nothing amiss here. McGuire can open to the public whenever he wants."

"Excellent," the mayor said in his booming voice. The two politicians went back to the stage and down into the auditorium to talk some more with McGuire and the men surrounding him.

Fargo wiped sweat from his forehead. He fought with fists and knives and guns. Doing it with woods was a mite harder, especially when dealing with a weasel like Trevor.

"I've seen 'em come and go," Reggie said. "I'd as soon see Trevor go and stay gone!"

"And he's one of the honest political appointees at City Hall," Watkins said knowingly. Seeing both Fargo and Reggie's expressions, he laughed and added. "He stays bought if you pay him off."

"As long as McGuire doesn't pay him off in flesh," Fargo said.

"Who is demanding a pound of flesh?" asked Amanda. "I wasn't aware that you knew *The Merchant of Venice*, Skye. 'Take then thy bond, take thou thy pound of flesh,' " quoted Amanda.

"Reggie was telling me all about it," Fargo said, grinning.

"Had a Shakespearean actor or two when I ran my own theater," Reggie said. "They was always goin' around quotin' stuff. Never had this Shylock play."

"Then how, oh, never mind," Amanda said airily. "Come along, Skye. You should take me to dinner. I need something to replenish my strength after all that effort onstage. It does so take it out of me, you understand."

"I can imagine," Willie Watkins said.

"Why don't you come along, too, Mr. Watkins?" Amanda asked unexpectedly, her gaze fixed on him.

Fargo felt a little uneasy about the way Amanda so freely invited people along. He was running short of money. Getting any from McGuire for the work he did wasn't likely, and the few dollars he had received in reward for saving the Butterfield shipment was about gone.

"Let's eat at the hotel," Amanda said. "Their café is so . . . quaint."

"How's that?" Watkins asked, as if he intended putting everything Amanda said into an article for his newspaper.

Fargo hung back to speak with Reggie.

"Did you see anyone poking around during the performance?" Fargo asked. "I don't mean the politicians."

"Ducks?" Reggie asked. He spat and accurately hit the cuspidor. "Nope, haven't seen hide nor hair of them since the fire. You run them varmints off?"

"I'm not betting on it," Fargo said. "I'd better catch up with Amanda and Watkins before they get into trouble."

"You see that, too, eh?" Reggie said. This stopped Fargo dead in his tracks. He stared at the old man. "Go on, now," urged Reggie. "Run along. I can look after the old theater by myself. Might even have a shot or two at Trevor, if that son of a buck pokes his head back in."

"Don't aim for the heart," Fargo said. "He doesn't look like the kind to have one."

"It'd be withered and black and small," argued Reggie. He pushed Fargo out the door and slammed the stage door behind him.

Fargo took a deep breath, got a mixture of burned wood and salt air into his lungs, then set out after Amanda and Watkins. He wished the actress had waited for him, but figured she was safe enough with Watkins.

He was wrong.

Fargo broke into a run and reached the end of the block where a smallish man in a cutaway coat had pushed Watkins to one side and backed Amanda into a wall. The man's top hat was knocked askew and when he reached inside his coat, Fargo drew his six-shooter and took aim.

"Hold on, mister!" Fargo barked. "Move a muscle and I'll shoot!"

The small man jumped as if Fargo had stuck him with a pin. His hand came out of an inner pocket holding a brown envelope.

"Skye, put that away," Amanda said. Her tone told him she was not afraid of any harm coming to her. He slipped his six-gun into its holster and came to stand beside her. He glared down at the small man.

"My offer, Miss Fredericks," the man said, handing over the envelope. Fargo started to take it, but Amanda beat him to it.

"This is so unexpected, Mr. Zinser."

"It is a generous offer, and we both know that poseur McGuire cannot match it. Your name will be five feet high on my marquee! I will commission plays written solely for you!"

"You're trying to steal her away from McGuire?" Fargo asked. He had not expected this.

"I will do more than try! I will succeed! Her name will be on the tongue of everyone in San Francisco! They will speak of Amanda Fredericks for a hundred years. A thousand!"

"I will look over your offer, Mr. Zinser, and let you know."

"It is the most generous offer you will get in this tight-fisted town," Zinser warned.

"Thank you for your kind words," Amanda said, looking at Watkins. The reporter stepped between her and the rival theater owner.

"May I publish the details of your offer, Mr. Zinser? I'm doing a series of stories on the arts in San Francisco."

"A reporter?" Zinser wrinkled his nose. "Your kind has not been generous to my performers. But with Miss Fredericks starring nightly, even those of lesser discrimination will see how grand her work is in my theater!"

Fargo moved beside Watkins and cut the small man off from Amanda entirely. He hustled Amanda along the street to get her away from the predatory theater owner.

"It's ever so flattering to have them making such fine speeches," Amanda said. She took Skye's arm and then locked her other through Watkins's. "How much do you think Zinser is offering?"

"I'd advise against jumping ship right now, Amanda," Fargo said. "Stay with McGuire, at least until your current play has a good run."

"Always loyal," the blonde said, smiling. "That's what I like about you, Skye. Your constancy rivals that of the stars in the heavens."

"I don't owe McGuire anything," Fargo said. "If you back out of *East Lynne*, McGuire will lose the Montgomery Street Melodeon, though. Why kick him while he's down, after he went to such lengths to bring you to town?"

"Loyal and kindhearted," Amanda said.

"But you have to look to your own financial well-being," Watkins said hastily. "Since your manager was killed, who has been shepherding your finances, Miss Fredericks?"

"Oh, call me Amanda. And there has not been any call to worry about such things, though Mr. McGuire must be straining to pay for his renovations because he insists on paying me after every performance. Fancy that."

"It might be best if you went to another theater," Watkins said. "Wait, Mr. Fargo. Hear me out. If she went to another theater, the Sydney Ducks would stop their attacks on her Their feud is with McGuire, not her."

Fargo thought about this. While it irked him to think Amanda was seriously considering Zinser's offer—he *was* disposed toward finishing what he started and expected others to do so, too—Willie Watkins had a good point. Amanda's safety was in doubt every time she walked out onto McGuire's stage.

"Did you sign a contract with McGuire?" he asked.

"Of course I did," Amanda said. "But I have no idea where my copy is. Randolph dealt with Mr. McGuire."

"And he's dead." Seeing Watkins's confusion, Fargo said, "Randolph Setts was Amanda's manager."

"He was the one killed during your stagecoach trip here," Watkins said, reaching for his notebook to make more cryptic inscriptions as they walked. "So you have no idea what terms Mr. Setts agreed to with McGuire?"

Fargo let the two discuss the legalities of Amanda simply leaving McGuire to accept Zinser's offer. He began looking ahead to where a small knot of well-dressed men waited on the sidewalk, obviously anticipating Amanda's arrival.

"Watkins, who are the men ahead?"

"More theater owners. At least, I recognize three of them as owning melodeons and dance halls. The others look even more prosperous and might be their financiers. Yes, that's Mr. Ralston, an up-and-coming banker."

Fargo prepared for a new barrage of offers for Amanda to work for other playhouse proprietors. His stride lengthened so he would be in front of her, able to block the men from her if the need arose. She released his arm and half-turned toward Watkins.

"Fargo!" the reporter shouted.

Faster than thought, Fargo spun and recognized the danger. A man came from the mouth of an alley just behind him. Fargo had been too intent on the theater owners to notice the man lurking in the shadows.

Fargo heard a gunshot, then realized it was a report from his own six-shooter. He had fired on instinct. The man who had lunged forward screamed as Fargo's bullet broke a glass jar in his hands, spattering his face and hands with the contents.

The sizzle of flesh burning told Fargo the jar had been filled with acid. Acid intended for Amanda.

15

Two screams rose and mingled in the air. The men on the sidewalk in front of Fargo froze at the soul-rending sound, but Watkins did not. He wrapped his arms around a shrieking Amanda, swung about and carried her back in the direction they had come, leaving Fargo free to deal with the man clawing at his face.

Fargo shoved the man into the alley so hard he lost his balance and crashed to the ground.

"Me face. I'm blind! You blinded me!"

"You tried to throw the acid in Miss Fredericks's face," Fargo said, standing over the man. His six-shooter still smoked from the single shot that had broken the jar containing the deadly fluid. It would take only a little pressure on the trigger to fire another bullet and end this foul acid-thrower's life. The tendons in Fargo's forearm stood out, then he relaxed. "Who sent you?"

"Me skin's burnin' off!" The man moaned pitifully, beginning to whimper after a few more seconds. Fargo felt no pity for him.

"Was it Clay Nance?"

"Yeah, he tole me to do it. He didn't mean nuthin' by it. This is jist business." The man had stopped clawing his face and rolled onto his side, his hands hidden under his coat.

Fargo fired once, twice, a third time.

"My God, man, you murdered him!" cried the well-dressed man who had finally ventured into the alley to see what had caused the ruckus. "He might have been a vile . . ." The words trailed off when Fargo put his boot to the dead man's side and pushed hard, rolling the Sydney Duck onto his back.

Clutched in his hand was a small four-barreled pistol.

"He would have shot me. The acid burned him, but not that badly. He used that to sucker me into thinking he was helpless."

Fargo left the man gawking at the body and went to the mouth of the alley. Several uniformed policemen rushed toward Fargo. One grabbed his six-shooter and shoved him against the wall while his comrades rushed to the fallen man.

"Dead, Sarge!" called one officer, kneeling by the body. "Three shots, right through the heart. Damn fine shooting."

"You're under arrest for murder. We don't allow none of that in San Francisco." The police sergeant pulled shackles from his pocket and started to put them on Fargo's wrists. Fargo pulled away and almost bolted. Since coming to town, he had contended with this upside-down justice constantly. But he was not going to give up easily if it meant going to jail where Nance might turn him into a sitting duck.

"Wait," said the man who had seen Fargo shoot the acid thrower. "I'm Major Defoe, and I am an eyewitness to this dastardly misconduct. The man you so wrongly accuse is a hero, not a criminal"

"Major Defoe?" asked the police sergeant. The policeman frowned in concentration as he fumbled in his uniform jacket pocket, drew out a notebook and leafed quickly through the pages. His eyes widened a little when he found a notation on a page toward the back of the book. "Sir, sorry about this trouble. We'll get rid of the body."

"Dump him into the bay for all I care," Defoe said tartly. "But you will apologize to this gentleman before doing anything." He held out his hand for Fargo to shake. "You've done us all a service, sir."

"Thanks," Fargo said. "I was just protecting myself."

"I think it was more than that, eh?" Defoe nudged him in the ribs as the police dragged away the body, a policeman holding each of the dead man's legs. "You were protecting Miss Fredericks, weren't you?"

Fargo saw no reason to answer when his motive was so obvious. He looked over his shoulder and saw Willie Watkins still calming Amanda's ruffled nerves.

"Well done, sir, very well done. I wouldn't want anything to happen to her because I want her to star in a new play at my melodeon. The Pacific Gentry Theater on Kearny Street. I am sure you've heard of it. Perhaps you and Miss Fredericks would care to come by later so we can discuss employment." Defoe cleared his throat, saw Fargo's disapproving look and hastily added, "For both of you, naturally."

"Naturally," Fargo said dryly. He took the business card Defoe thrust at him, then watched the rival theater owner like a hawk as he paid his respects to Amanda. Fargo laughed when he saw how protective Watkins had become, putting himself between Amanda and Defoe, acting like a sheepdog protecting his flock from a wolf.

When Defoe strutted off, whistling a jaunty tune, Fargo went to see how Amanda was faring.

"Oh, Skye, how terrible!" cried Amanda. She threw her arms around his neck and hugged him tightly. Her body quaked in reaction to her close call with disfigurement.

"This is the straw that broke the camel's back," Watkins said hotly. "Nance is stooping lower and lower. It's one thing to try to kill someone, but it's another to try to ruin such beauty."

"What do you suggest doing?" asked Fargo, his arms still around Amanda. She wasn't shaking as badly, and was regaining her usual pluck. He released her and she stepped away, dabbing at her eyes.

"No damage done, except to my nerves," Amanda said. "You were so brave. Both of you."

"I need to talk to McGuire about what he owes Nance," Fargo said. "Willie can look after you for a while."

"Sure, Fargo, be glad to," Watkins said quickly. "We were going to get some dinner. Is that all right, Miss Fredericks? Are you still hungry? It'd take your mind off this horrible attack."

"Please, call me Amanda," the blonde actress said, smiling at the reporter. She took his arm, but her gray eyes were on Fargo as they walked off.

Fargo watched until they went into a restaurant a block off, then went to lay out the way it had to be with Horatio McGuire. Watkins was right about one thing. The attacks had to stop. Now.

A cold wind from the direction of the bay insinuated itself through cracks in the theater walls as Fargo hunted for McGuire. The portly theater owner sat behind his desk in his office, stacks of paper around him. He looked up, a harassed expression on his face.

"Mr. Fargo. What do you want?"

"A truce between you and Nance," Fargo said. "I'd like to see the son of a bitch dead, but tracking him down is a problem. Since it isn't likely the two of us will settle our personal feud, you've got to make your peace with him."

"Why? Isn't it enough I have bills stacked to the ceiling? How can I pay him a single penny when all this is weighing me down like a boat anchor? And you are making me pay Miss Fredericks after every performance. Do you know how hard that is?" McGuire raged on about his high overhead and lack of money. Then Fargo told him what had happened to Amanda.

"She's all right?" McGuire looked as if he might have a heart attack at the thought of losing his star attraction.

"She'll have a happier future if you and the Sydney Ducks aren't feuding. Pay back the money Nance loaned you, with the interest. That ought to end his attacks."

"How? The theater won't open for a few more days, and the bills! I have so many bills!" McGuire tore at his sparse hair and his dewlaps bounced as his agitation mounted.

"You'll never pay off a cent of any of this if Amanda is dead or permanently disfigured," Fargo said. "Get some of your new friends to loan you the money. You and the mayor are getting on well. He has connections with the bankers.

"There's that upstart Ralston," McGuire said, a forefinger pressed into his lips as he thought. "He fancies himself one of the elite and might lend me a few dollars for the entrée to society it would give him and his gold digger of a wife."

"Cut him in as part owner, if need be," Fargo said. "You have to find some way to deal with Nance."

Fargo wondered what he would do when Nance called off his war with McGuire. All he had done was deliver Arthur Nance's legacy; and had found himself in a pit filled with vipers—and they all looked like Clay Nance. Before coming to San Francisco, he had no idea that Nance was involved with the Sydney Ducks, but somehow the Ducks' leader had made Fargo a personal obsession.

Or was that the other way around? Had Fargo made Nance his own obsession because of his attacks on Amanda? It was getting to be time to leave San Francisco and the city-bred woes behind him. All he had to do was pour oil on troubled waters, be sure Amanda was safe, and then he could ride for the high country again.

"I'll do what I can," McGuire said. "I owe it to my staff, to Miss Fredericks, to the arts!"

Fargo knew what McGuire meant, and it had nothing to do with benefitting the world of performing theater. He was going to be very happy to ride away from San Francisco.

"He wouldn't accept the deal, Fargo," complained McGuire. "I had it all. Every last dime and even the usurious interest Nance charged. It was a pretty pile of money, believe me. In gold. It was in gold!"

"What happened?" Fargo asked. He did not like the way McGuire had turned red in the face when discussing Nance and the money. The theater owner fidgeted and kept his eyes averted as he ranted.

"He took the money. All I owed him, including the interest and—"

"What *happened*?" Fargo was losing patience. Something had gone wrong, and McGuire was fluttering around facing up to it.

"He took the money and still demanded more. I told you how he tried to extort me before."

"Paying a man money he's owed isn't extortion," Fargo pointed out.

"This is. Nance took the money and said I had to keep paying. A hundred dollars every week or else there would be hell to pay."

"Did he threaten Amanda?"

"Not in so many words. He said I had to let him be a silent partner. Imagine me giving him any part of the Montgomery Street Melodeon!" McGuire quieted a little. "Besides, I can't do that. I had to take on three partners to raise Nance's money. There would be nothing left for me if I gave him even a small percent of the theater."

Fargo knew better than to think Nance's extortion threats were only bravado.

"I wanted to be here when you talked to him. Why didn't you let me know when you were meeting him?"

"I . . . he told me not to. I didn't think there was anything wrong with such an arrangement. There was only supposed to be the two of us, but he double-crossed me and came with four henchmen. The Ducks are a vicious lot. All Australian killers. They—"

"What are you going to do?"

"The theater's grand reopening is tonight. If all goes well, he might carry through on his threats."

"You figure he wants everyone to know what the Sydney Ducks can do?" Fargo nodded. This made sense. Nance had ambitions far beyond shaking down Horatio McGuire. If his extortion worked for one theater, it would work for others. Every eye in San Francisco would be turned toward the Montgomery Street Melodeon's reopening with Amanda onstage in what Fargo had seen described in the newspapers as the finest play ever written by a local writer.

"We have to get through the night somehow without Nance burning down the theater," McGuire said.

"Or harming Amanda or any of the cast," Fargo said.

"Yes, yes, that goes without saying. What can you do?"

"What I've been doing. I'll watch Amanda, but I have a

gut feeling that Nance has something in mind even worse than harming her. He didn't succeed in burning down the theater and the acid-thrower got a few slugs pumped into his heart."

"What else can he do?" McGuire looked as if he had bitten into an apple and found half a worm.

Fargo shrugged and shook his head. He had no idea what Nance would do, but he would lay a hefty bet that it would be something nasty, public, and flashy. He left McGuire's office, made a quick circuit through the newly repainted theater, and found nothing amiss, then went to Amanda's dressing room. It looked as if she was holding a rehearsal there as most of the cast had crowded in.

"We will be wonderful tonight," Amanda said to the cast members. "There will be a new radiance in San Francisco, and it will come from this very theater. We will shine!"

"Make sure that reporter friend of yours says that," an older actor said.

"Make sure he gets our names right this time," complained another. "He didn't even spell *Richelieu* right and it was up there on the marquee for him to copy letter for letter."

"That's not as bad as the way he ignored us entirely when he reported on the show we gave for the politicians," chimed in a mousy-looking actress.

"Oh, you do go on so," laughed Amanda. If another had laughed like that, blood would have been spilled. Somehow, Amanda turned it into an intimate friendly sharing rather than derision. Fargo stepped aside as the cast filed out, mumbling among themselves as they prepared for the opening curtain.

"Skye, darling, come in and close the door. They are such children! I had to buoy their spirits." Amanda waved as if shooing way flies. "It's only opening night jitters, although this is hardly our opening."

"Has McGuire talked to you about Nance?" he asked.

"Why, no. The way he talked, it was all taken care of, though how that is possible, short of that horrid man being in jail, is beyond me." Amanda applied her heavy makeup as she spoke. Fargo saw her attention was directed to the upcoming play and nothing else. He left her talking to herself, and she did not take notice.

Outside her dressing room, Fargo called Reggie over. The old man hobbled a little tonight.

"It's nothin' that'll slow down this old warhorse, Fargo," Reggie said, seeing his concern. "I'm as quick on the draw as I ever was." To show his prowess, Reggie whipped out his two six-shooters and had them cocked before Fargo could tell him not to bother.

"Watch her," Fargo said. "I'm going to see what mischief Nance is really up to."

"You don't think he'll try to hurt her during the play, do you?"

"Nance is cagier than that. The public outcry would make things too hot for him and the Ducks. Whatever he does won't appear to be his doing, but everyone will know who is responsible."

"How do you stop something you can't put into words," mused Reggie. "That's a tall chore."

Fargo laughed ruefully. It was more than that. It might be impossible. He checked the wings and saw the stagehands beginning their preparations. Already a few of the audience were trickling in to get good seats up close to the stage. Fargo eyed them closely, decided they were only eager patrons and nothing more, then made his way up to the balcony box seats. McGuire's wealthier and more favored patrons were situating themselves already. Fargo kept moving until he got to the main lobby.

From outside came a low rumble from the crowd, as if it were a pot on the verge of boiling.

"What's wrong?" Fargo asked McGuire. The rotund theater owner mopped his forehead with a handkerchief. Something was not going the way it should.

"I let in a few select people, and the rest want in, too."

"If they've got tickets, let them in," Fargo said. "There's no reason to keep them locked out. Think of the extra liquor you'll peddle." The words had barely left his lips when he heard a loud cry go up at the rear of the crowd.

Angry words were exchanged and soon it seemed as if everyone outside the theater was caught in the middle of a fistfight.

Fargo pushed through one door, shoved away a man who tried to get in before he could close it behind him, and then looked over the undulating sea of heads. Most of the people stirred uneasily, not sure what was happening. Fargo quickly located the trouble at the fringes of the crowd and made his way out. An unkempt man had picked a fight with a more prosperous citizen.

"Yer nothin' but a pus-runnin' canker sore, you dumb son of a bitch!" yelled the slovenly man, shoving the other so hard he fell to the street. "Come on, be a man. Fight! Or are you too lily-livered fer that? Come on now, mate!" He drew back his fist and waited for the man he had shoved down to stand so he could knock him down again.

Fargo caught the man's cocked fist and spun him around.

"Leave him alone," Fargo said coldly. "You don't have a quarrel with anyone here."

"I got one with you!" The man tried to hit Fargo with his free hand. Fargo avoided the clumsy blow, twisted hard, and crushed down on the wrist he still held imprisoned in his strong grip. The man yelped in pain as Fargo broke his arm and drove him to the ground. Fargo dropped on top of him, a knee in his gut.

"You work for Nance, don't you? You're a Duck."

"Go to hell!" the man spat out.

Fargo leaned forward, his knee going deeper into the man's gut. A quick punch put out the Sydney Duck's lights. But Fargo heard other fights breaking out all around. Nance had sent a handful of his men to start arguments wherever they could. It might drive away patrons from the Montgomery Street Melodeon, or leave them with such a distaste that they would never return.

Either way, Nance would hurt McGuire's business.

Figuring out who were the troublemakers and who were the paying customers proved easier than stopping the fights. Fargo moved as fast as he could around the edge of the crowd where the Sydney Ducks incited the brawls, hoping a few fistfights would become a donnybook. It required the use of his six-gun to buffalo more than one of the agitators, but the crowd began to settle down a mite.

Until a sudden collective cheer went up. Fargo was almost trampled when McGuire finally opened the doors and let in the expectant crowd. He was buffeted around and then found himself on the street surrounded by the half dozen unconscious Sydney Ducks he had laid out in his attempt to keep the peace.

He wished some of the policemen would come along, but, like the Specials, they steered clear of anything that might put life and limb in jeopardy. Fargo began dragging the unconscious Ducks to the alley behind the theater. When he had finished, he had a pile six Ducks deep at the foot of the stairs leading backstage.

Fargo rapped on the door, then waited until Reggie opened it a crack and saw who stood there.

"What you been up to, Fargo? The buzz in the crowd 'bout what's been happenin' out front is an ugly one."

"Nothing to worry about," Fargo said. "I need some help moving trash out back."

"Moving them varmints?" Reggie asked, looking past Fargo to the pile of Sydney Ducks in the alley. "Hell, I'll get a couple of stagehands 'n we kin dump 'em in the bay. Or maybe I kin think of somethin' even more pleasin' that'll keep 'em outta our hair for a long, long time."

"A good idea," Fargo said. "I'd help, but I want to be sure none of their buddies are in the crowd."

"Miss Fredericks—" Reggie began.

"I don't think so. They want to stir up trouble in the audience, not hurt her." Fargo silently added, "I hope."

Reggie went to get help—men more used to moving scenery. One brought around a wagon, and they loaded the Ducks in the back. Fargo watched as Reggie rattled off, his cargo beginning to stir, and wondered if the old man could handle the hoodlums. With the other stagehands, he decided Reggie was more than capable of finishing the chore.

He slammed and barred the stage door and went to the wings to deal with the next emergency when he heard

Willie Watkins begin to shout Amanda's name. The audience took up the cheer and the curtain rose to even greater applause.

For better or worse, the play had begun.

16

"On the way to the bay to dump that load of garbage, I had an idea," Reggie said, looking proud of himself. "There were three China Clippers in port, ready to sail on the morning tide."

"So?" asked Fargo, distracted and feeling as nervous as a long-tailed cat laying next to a rocking chair. Amanda's nearly finished performance was lackluster and flat. The acid-throwing incident had shaken her, but she had snapped back. Yet for some reason, the fights before the audience got into the theater bothered her enough to affect her acting now.

"You ain't from these parts," Reggie said, "so you don't know how captains get their crew. It's called shanghaiing, since that's where most all the ships are bound."

"You gave the Sydney Ducks to a captain to be in his crew?" Fargo's entire attention focused on Reggie now. "They'll be gone for months and months."

"Maybe longer, if they don't snap to and work dang hard. One captain's got a reputation of being a real martinet. And nope, I didn't give the Ducks to anybody. I *sold* them." Reggie pulled out a sheaf of currency and riffled through it. "You want half?" The old man sounded hesitant about the offer.

Fargo shook his head. He wanted no part of money tainted by impressment. That struck him as a fancy name for slavery. The Ducks deserved punishment, but selling them as part of a ship's crew might not have been the proper thing to do, even if the San Francisco authorities were not inclined to prosecute them for their crimes.

"Thanks, I kin use the money. You've noticed how much of a tightwad McGuire is. I swear he'll be put into the grave squeezing the first dime he ever stole." Reggie tucked the money into his pocket, peered around the curtain at Amanda, and looked a little sad at what he saw.

"She's off her feed today," Reggie said. "It happens. They got a sayin' in the theater. Good rehearsal, bad show."

"I hope she can forget everything but the play," Fargo said. "Nance is going to be forced to do something now that he's lost a half dozen of his gang."

"He won't notice," Reggie assured him. "The Sydney Ducks are not like a family. Leastwise no family I ever heard of. More like they are all feuding with each other all the time."

Fargo wanted to believe that, but knew better. Clay Nance would devote more and more of his time to pressuring McGuire into paying his extortion money. To do anything else would jeopardize his position as leader of the Ducks.

"You watch her, will you, Reggie? There are a few men in the back of the theater talking with McGuire, so he's not going to be on the lookout for trouble."

"Get yourself some chow, Fargo," the old man said. "I'll look after her for you."

Fargo let the stage door close behind him and waited for Reggie to bar it. He went down the steps to see Willie Watkins walking briskly in his direction. Even he didn't have the heart to finish watching Amanda's sorry performance.

"Mr. Fargo! Just the man I wanted to see!"

"Why's that?" Fargo asked. Watkins fell into step with him and walked to Montgomery Street in front of the theater.

"The editor is going to print my first story. The one detailing how we ventured into Sydney-Town! I'm going to be on the staff."

"I thought you already were," Fargo said, heading for a café down the block.

"Reporting social events and theater openings isn't real reporting," Watkins said pompously. "But this is! When can we go back? I need to learn more about the Sydney Ducks. I can tell everything about their leaders, how they operate, what a crooked bunch they are!"

"Settle down," Fargo advised. "You know all that. Why go back and taunt Nance?"

"Maybe I like dancing close to the flames," Watkins said.

"Maybe you like getting blisters on your feet," Fargo shot back. He started to go into the restaurant, then went a few paces past and stopped. He was about as broke as a man could be. Earlier, he had avoided the embarrassment of not being able to pay for Amanda's and his own meal because the acid-thrower had created a diversion. Food had been forgotten afterward.

"Where are you going, Mr. Fargo? We need to talk."

"Then you're buying my meal," Fargo said.

"I have an expense account now that I'm a full-fledged reporter," Watkins said proudly.

"That café looks as good as any," Fargo said, reversing his course to return to the restaurant. He stopped and stared hard at a man who had been following them. The man flipped up his collar, whirled around, and almost ran off.

"What's wrong?" asked Watkins.

"Nothing," Fargo said, seeing the man who had acted so suspiciously vanish around the next corner. He was jumping at shadows. Nance was not constantly spying on him. To think that was to give the Sydney Ducks' leader the upper hand and wear himself out.

They sat at a table in one corner of the small dining room, Fargo with his back to the wall. He had a good view out the large plate-glass window into the street so he could watch the bustle of theatergoers on their way to any number of plays in the area. Fargo hoped Amanda's performance improved, or McGuire might have to shut down his theater on the night that he had planned for a major triumph.

"Steak for my friend," Watkins said grandly. "I'll have a cup of coffee."

"Coffee, also," Fargo said, amused at Watkins. The young reporter was still feeling out the limits of his new job. He was willing to spend a dollar for a steak for Fargo, but wasn't going to eat anything himself. Fargo didn't much care if Watkins walked in constant fear of his city editor. The smell of food made his mouth water, and his belly actually believe his throat had not been cut.

As he ate, he listened with half an ear to Watkins ramble about the hard-hitting stories he would write, making the mayor realize the threat the Sydney Ducks posed to San Francisco.

"Don't you think he already knows?" asked Fargo, to keep Watkins talking so he could keep eating. Nobody in political power stayed there by being stupid or foolish. Van Ness knew the full extent of Clay Nance's power and was probably being paid off to look the other way. If Watkins wanted to change that, he had to make it more worthwhile for the mayor to crack down on the gang. That might mean an uprising of citizens or even the formation of yet another vigilance committee. But Watkins was going to be mighty disappointed if he thought a single story would shake up the way things were.

Fargo hesitated, a piece of steak halfway to his mouth, when he saw a man silhouetted in the doorway. The light from the gas streetlamp plunged the man's features into shadow, but something about him was familiar.

It came to Fargo about the same time he saw the flare of a lucifer and the sputtering fuse disappearing into a lead pipe.

"Get down!" Fargo shouted, upending he able and pushing Watkins to one side.

The man in the doorway tossed the crude bomb underhand in Fargo's direction, then ducked out. Fargo's fingers were still locked on the edge of the table. He jerked around and dropped the table onto the bomb as it went off. For a moment, Fargo thought nothing had happened. Then he felt himself lifted off his feet and thrown back into the wall. He smashed into the wall hard, then slid down, stunned.

He shook off the shock of the explosion and looked around the small restaurant. Others were as shaken as he was, but no one seemed to be hurt.

"Watkins?" he called, not seeing the young reporter. "Where are you?" Fargo fought to get to his feet. Unsteadily, he pushed through a forest of shattered chairs and the debris left of the table to find Willie Watkins.

"What happened?" the reporter moaned. He put his hand to his forehead and it came away bloody. "My God, I've been killed!"

"You haven't been killed," Fargo said, "but not through lack of trying."

"A bomb," Watkins said, smearing more blood off his forehead. A nasty gash was making him bleed like a stuck pig. Fargo grabbed a napkin and pressed it to the wound.

"Hold that tight," Fargo advised. He looked around the café to be sure no one else had been seriously injured by the bomb meant for him. While stunned, the other patrons were moving about and were none the worse for wear.

Fargo put his arm around Watkins's shoulders and got the reporter to his feet. They went to the front of the restaurant. Rather than leaving through the doorway, which had been destroyed by the blast, Fargo went through the shattered window. Glass grating under his boots, he helped Watkins to the sidewalk.

"Where are we going?" Watkins asked, more dazed now than he had been immediately after the blast.

"I need to get you to a doctor," Fargo said. "Where do I find one?" He looked around as he spoke to be sure that the bomber was not waiting to finish the job. The heavy stench of partly burned powder hung in the air. The Duck needed to learn better blasting techniques if he wanted to use bombs to get the men Nance ordered killed.

"Skye, Willie, are you all right? Oh, no!" cried Amanda, hurrying over. "I heard an explosion as we all came out to get some food after the performance. Are you hurt?" She pried Watkins's hand away so she could look at the cut.

Fargo wasn't sure what he expected from the actress. Histrionics perhaps, but not the no-nonsense attitude she showed now, especially after what had to be a disappointing performance onstage.

"It's not bad. You don't need a doctor for this. Help me get him to the hotel, Skye. I can tend to him there, but we'd better go up the back way. The doorman is not likely to let in anyone this disreputable looking."

"Me, disreputable?" asked Watkins, trying to make it sound like a joke. His legs buckled under him, but Fargo caught him before he hit the sidewalk. Amanda summoned a carriage and they went to the rear of the hotel where Fargo struggled to get a barely conscious Watkins up the stairs.

"I have this now," Amanda said, holding up a key. "I sweet-talked it out of the room clerk." She used the key to open the door Fargo had jimmied before. It was only a short way down the corridor to Amanda's room, but Watkins proved deadweight by the time they reached it.

"Put him on the bed," she ordered.

"He's going to bleed on the bedspread," Fargo said. "The cut's not serious, but stopping it from gushing all over the place is going to be a chore."

"Don't worry about that, Skye. For what McGuire's paying for this room, they cannot complain about a little matter like a stained bedspread. Or even the demolished door." Amanda grinned when she pointed to the repaired doorframe he had shouldered through when Desirée's hired killers had kidnapped her.

Fargo watched as Amanda expertly cut strips from a petticoat and bandaged Watkins's gash. She laid a hand on his cheek almost lovingly, then took it away.

"No fever," she said, smiling.

"Where did you learn to nurse like that?" Fargo asked, impressed with her cool efficiency. He had not expected her to go into a faint, but he had not expected her to be so adroit at patching up a wound, either.

"I played a nurse in a play once," she said. "See? The theater can be very educational."

Fargo wasn't sure if she was making fun of him.

"Come and sit beside me, Skye," she said, taking his hand and pulling him toward the chair by the dresser. Since there wasn't room for both of them on the chair, she pushed him down, then sat in his lap. She wiggled a little and settled herself. The pressure of her bottom across his crotch made Fargo remember another of the things he liked so much about Amanda.

She was one sexy woman.

"I'm as dirty as Watkins," Fargo said.

"You worry about such silly things," Amanda said, her face close to his. She put her arms around his neck to balance herself. "What happened? Tell me every detail."

As Fargo talked, he felt the way the alluring blonde began wiggling. The story was exciting her.

"So you both could have been killed?" she said in a husky whisper. "You're so brave."

Fargo didn't look at it that way. He had done what little he could to keep the bomb from killing everyone in the café, himself included. Dropping the heavy wooden table on top of the pipe had been the only thing he could do—and it had worked. That didn't make him brave as much as it did lucky.

"You should be rewarded for saving Willie and all the other people," Amanda said, shifting a little more in his lap. Their lips were only inches apart. And then they were locked together in a passionate kiss that robbed both of them of their breath.

"What about Watkins?" Fargo asked, trying to look past her.

"He's sleeping so hard it'd take a cannon blast to wake him up."

"Might be we end up waking him up, if that's all it takes." Fargo said.

"Let's try!"

Fargo found himself yearning for Amanda and all she was so wantonly offering. The nearness of death made him even more appreciative of life. And for her this was a way of forgetting her poor performance onstage. Amanda's breasts crushed warmly against his chest as his arms encircled her and pulled her closer.

They kissed for long minutes, then let their tongues begin tentative explorations of each other's mouths. Fargo's hands roved up and down Amanda's back, finding tiny ribbons holding together her clothing. By the time they were both breathless from kissing, he had her blouse partly pulled away from her silky-skinned body.

"Wait, Skye," she said, shucking off the top of her dress and standing naked to the waist in front of him. She reached down and began tugging at his pants. He hastily pushed them down and let out his raging manhood.

Amanda smiled wickedly at the sight of the erect shaft. She ran her fingers up and down its length a few times and got it steely hard.

"That's the way I like it," she said in a sexy voice.

"And this is the way I like it," Fargo said, his hands reaching under her skirts and lifting them. His fingertips danced along the sleekness of her legs, touching her hips and then slipping to her inner thighs. He parted her legs as she bent forward over him.

Her turgid nipples came within reach of his mouth. They were too succulent a treat to ignore. Fargo sucked first one and then the other, using both tongue and teeth to stimulate her even more. Amanda gasped in delight when he sucked in one rock-hard nipple, caught it between his teeth, and then pushed it free with his tongue. He repeated the oral assault on her other breast.

The blonde went weak in the knees and sank forward, straddling his legs. With his hands between her legs, he was in perfect position to reach up, caress her fleece-covered nether lips, and feel the dampness seeping from her molten core.

"Yes, Skye, there, oh yes, I love it so! You're so big!" She inched forward a little more, then sat down hard. He guided his shaft into her as she sank across his lap.

For a moment, they simply sat and relished the sensations rippling through their bodies. Then this simple pleasure was no longer enough. Amanda rose a few inches and let his fleshy pillar slip out of her clutching female sheath. When only the slick head of his shaft remained inside her, she paused, twisted from side to side, then collapsed, taking him in a rush.

Fargo gasped as the clinging warmth surrounded him once more. He stroked up and down the woman's back, tracing out each and every bone in her spine. His touch caused her to tremble. She lifted up off his lap and shoved her chest forward again. He took a second sample of her twin cherry-sized nipples, his hands sneaking back under her flowing skirts. This time he cupped her fleshy buttocks.

"Oh, Skye, so nice," Amanda cooed.

"What?" he asked. "This?" He nibbled at her breasts. "Or this?" He twisted hard on the twin handfuls of backside. When he kneaded and massaged her rump, her inner muscles tensed and clamped down on the thick head of his manhood.

"Both," she said. "But I can do something for you, too." Amanda sank down slowly. As she took him fully inside her again, he pressed her buttocks together. Fargo thought he was going to lose control. Her tensed inner walls clenched down like a delightful vise around him.

Fargo let his hands glide over the rounded buttocks but found himself increasingly distracted by the up-and-down action as the woman began pumping faster and faster. Amanda gasped and moaned until Fargo knew Watkins would wake up. By then he did not care. The heat from her striving body flowed down his length and into his loins. Fargo was coming to a boil from her eager, active movement.

When Amanda started lifting and dropping with seductive twists of her hips, Fargo was no longer able to restrain himself. With each hand he grabbed a handful of flesh and began guiding her rise and fall in a rhythm that set him on fire.

"Oh, yes, Skye, I—I—" Amanda groaned, closed her eyes and threw back her head. Long ash-blonde hair floated like a banner on the breeze as her breasts came within reach of his lips. He thrust out his tongue and dragged it over the turgid tips. This was all it took for the woman to explode in ecstacy. As the violent waves of passion blasted through her body, Fargo let go, too. Locked together, they rocked back and forth until the chair creaked ominously under their thrashing weights.

Amanda slowed her breakneck pace and finally sank down with her arms around his neck, hips no longer frenetically moving.

"So nice, Skye. You're just what I needed."

He kissed her, but knew there wouldn't be a second round now. From the direction of the bed came low moans as Willie Watkins rolled onto his side and pressed his forehead into the pillow.

"I have to go tend to Mr. Watkins," Amanda said, her gray eyes fixed on Fargo's lake-blue ones.

"Why not?" Fargo said. "You've just tended to me quite well."

Amanda smiled broadly, kissed him again, then wiggled back and stood, still naked to the waist. Fargo loved the way her breasts swayed as she moved. Then those sweet, plentiful mounds vanished as she hastily pulled on the blouse she had shed earlier.

In minutes, she sat beside Watkins and looked like the efficient nurse again. Fargo heaved a sigh and knew what he had to do now.

It would not be anywhere near as pleasant as the time he had just spent with Amanda.

17

Nance had the knack for turning invisible. If he had been hiding in the mountains or out on the plains, Fargo could have tracked him down eventually, but having to watch his back and worry about anyone he spoke to telling Nance that he had someone after him made a change of tactics necessary. Fargo headed in the direction of Sydney-Town, not especially hurrying.

A little after midnight, Fargo found himself a place to watch the Specials' headquarters and settled down to wait. He did not know if Hayworth still worked as a private policeman or if Nance had left him dead somewhere. It was even possible Hayworth had gone straightaway to the Sydney Ducks' leader and told him everything about the foray into Chinatown. Any promise Hayworth might have made about ratting on Nance would have been ignored, Fargo was positive.

He waited only an hour before Hayworth came bustling up the street with three other Specials. They stood in front of the building, arguing about something Fargo could not overhear. Hayworth eventually parted company with the others, who had gone into the headquarters.

Fargo wasted no time crossing the street and coming up behind Hayworth to catch him unawares.

"Don't turn around," Fargo said.

"You got a gun on me?" Hayworth almost jumped out of his skin. "Don't shoot me in the back!"

"You made a promise. Remember?" Fargo almost laughed when Hayworth hesitated. The Special worked over all the ways of weaseling out of the promise to help find Clay Nance in exchange for sparing his life.

"Whatcha want from me, Fargo?" Hayworth was almost whining now. "I can't go against Nance. You don't know how many men he's got runnin' with him."

"Scores of Sydney Ducks," Fargo said.

"At least!"

"I don't care if there're thousands. The time's come to put an end to the feud. He got his money from McGuire and has to call off his extortion."

"He won't, not that greedy bastard, not 'less he's dead," Hayworth said, starting to turn to face Fargo. Fargo put his hand on the Special's shoulder and kept him facing away. This gave Fargo a measure of control and added a tad of fear to the man's demeanor.

"Then he'll have to end up dead."

"Nance wants to muscle into the theater trade. He's seen how many people go to them fancy shows and how much money there is to be made. He thinks it's easy money for him and the Ducks."

Fargo had to convince Nance that it wasn't easy money.

"Where do I find him?"

"Look Fargo, it'll be my head if he finds out."

"Then you had better hope I don't make any mistakes. Where is Nance?"

"He . . . he moves around a lot." Hayworth hesitated, then added, "I'm surprised you're still alive and kickin'. I heard Nance sent a fellow to kill you. He didn't take kindly to havin' six of his gang shanghaied."

"It takes more than a bomb to kill me."

"I know a place where he might be."

"Tell me," Fargo said, looking around. Standing on the street had advantages. Hayworth wasn't as likely to try anything. The other side of the coin was the chance that a Sydney Duck might spot him and report back to Nance.

"Big poker game. You know Nance is a real gambler? There's a big game at a place called the Cobweb Palace. It's out on the piers, built right over the bay. Watch out for trapdoors that open up and dump you into the water. More 'n one man's met his end there, since they feed the sharks chum to keep them hanging around."

Fargo stepped back, ducked down an alley, and hurriedly cut through town until he was out of Sydney-Town and back into a safer section of San Francisco, if anywhere in town was safe as long as Nance carried on his squabble.

It was well past midnight when Fargo returned to the hotel, using the front door for the first time in ages. The doorman glared at him, telling Fargo he had worn out his welcome. With any luck—and even a hint of truth in what Hayworth had told him—he would clear out of town soon.

But first he had to stop Nance.

Fargo stopped in front of Amanda's door and started to knock. His hand went to his six-shooter when he saw the door was slightly ajar. He pushed it open with the toe of his boot, ready for anything but what he saw.

Amanda was stretched out beside Willie Watkins in bed. Both were naked and covered in sweat. He didn't have to ask what they had been doing. Fargo slowly closed the door to keep from disturbing them, ruefully reflecting on how he had warmed up the blonde actress for the reporter.

When he and Amanda had been together earlier, Fargo had felt a certain finality about it, but had thought it was more on his part than hers. He intended to move on soon. But she had beaten him to it.

Amanda was the kind of woman who needed variety in her life and had certainly gotten it from the rough-hewn Trailsman. He had given as good as he got, and there were no regrets.

Fargo spent the next hour making preparations for bearding Nance in his den of iniquity. The heavy early morning fog drifting in slowly off the bay reminded Fargo of a funeral shroud, but it also gave him some cover for what he wanted to do.

Around four o'clock he went to the end of the pier leading out to the Cobweb Palace, a disreputable shanty leaking light through the cracks in the walls. From inside came the muffled drone of men laughing, drinking, and fighting. Fargo looked around and knew he had been right making plans to safeguard himself. There was no escape except back in the direction he had come—and into the bay where curved gray fins restlessly cut the surface before vanishing silently, hidden by inky water and thick fog.

It was the sort of place that would appeal to the Sydney Ducks.

Fargo approached the Cobweb Palace warily, hunting for guards that Nance might have posted. The Sydney Ducks' leader must have felt secure here because Fargo saw no one until he pushed aside the canvas flap that served as a door. The thick smoke inside made him cough. Eyes stinging and watering, Fargo slipped along the outer wall so his back was always covered.

A parrot let out a shrill screech, dived from a perch in the cobwebby ceiling, and clawed at a sailor's face. The sailor recoiled and batted at the brightly plumed bird. The parrot vented a string of curses in a half dozen languages Fargo recognized, and several more he didn't. Then the bird hopped along the bar and helped itself to the booze left in the sailor's glass.

The sailor tried to squash the bird with his fist, but the barkeep was faster with a short club. He swung it viciously and caught the sailor in the middle of the face, breaking his nose and sending him staggering back into a table of cardplayers. When the sailor lost his balance and crashed into the table, chips and cards flew everywhere.

Fargo saw his chance and took it. When the gamblers made a grab for the sailor to throw him off their table, Fargo picked up as many of the chips on the floor as he could. He dodged the sailor's untimely exit as two bouncers picked the man up and threw him through the canvas flap onto the pier beyond.

Fargo continued moving through the room, snaring chips as he went because he had spotted Clay in the rear of the saloon. The man had a circle of his cronies around him and looked as permanent as any of the cobwebs or the fluently cursing drunken parrot.

He took a big gamble coming here, but Fargo knew he wasn't likely to run Nance to ground any other way. This was the Sydney Ducks' town, not his. Boldly walking to the table where Nance played a game of five-card stud, Fargo planted his feet and waited for the gambler to notice him.

Nance looked up only after one of the Sydney Ducks tried to push Fargo away and ended up screaming in pain with a broken arm.

"You got sand, I'll give you that," Clay Nance said. "What kind of funeral you want? Or will tossing you into the bay for the sharks be good enough?"

"Still letting everyone else to your dirty work, Nance?" Fargo asked. "How many Ducks have you lost trying to muscle in on McGuire? How many have you lost trying to kill me when you couldn't do it yourself?" Fargo tensed when three of the gang slipped hands into their pockets, all ready to pull weapons.

"What are you saying, Fargo?" demanded Nance.

"You—and he rest of your gang—know. You're a coward. You let others do your dirty work. Even worse, you're sending them to their deaths because you don't have the guts to face me yourself."

Fargo knew he had pushed Nance far enough. The leader of the Sydney Ducks spread his hands on the table, then moved his elbows closer to his body, as if he was going to launch himself across the table at Fargo.

"We can settle this once and for all with a single game," Fargo said. "If you're not afraid of losing."

Nance laughed and spread his hands out on the table in front of him again.

"Me, afraid of losing? I'm the best damned gambler in San Francisco. I know it and so do my boys here. Why should I get into a game with you when I can have you killed?"

"But you won't do it yourself, will you?" Fargo goaded.

"I'm not afraid of you," Nance said coldly.

"Prove it."

"I don't have to," Nance said, sneering.

"He's afraid of me," Fargo said, directing the words to the Sydney Ducks around Nance. "He sends you to do his dirty work and now he won't even play me in a game of cards. Do you really follow a man like this?"

"He's got a point, Clay," said the stockiest of the Sydney Ducks. "You been lettin' ever'one else go after him. Never saw no reason other 'n it's fun to beat up people. But Chance and Lee and Froggie, they never came back when you put them on 'im."

A murmur went around the table. Nance glared at Fargo, seeing he was losing his command over the tough gang.

"All right, Fargo. Draw poker. You got money or are you just blowing steam?" Nance shuffled a greasy deck of cards in front of him, never taking his eyes off Fargo.

Fargo tossed down the handful of chips he had collected making his way across the Cobweb Palace.

"We play until one of us is tapped out. Only what's on the table counts," Fargo said. He saw that Nance had five times as much as he did, but he had to keep the Sydney Ducks on his side with the audacious challenge to force Nance to call a truce. If he lost, he wasn't any worse off than before. But if he won . . .

"I can use your money. I'll buy whiskey for all my boys. And then I'll have them cut off your ears. What do you say to that?"

"I can use *your* money," Fargo countered. "When I win, you'll leave McGuire and everyone at his theater alone."

"I'll have the fat bastard for tea and eat his strumpet later because I'm gonna win," Nance said nastily, riffling through the cards. He did not offer Fargo a chance to cut the deck but dealt expertly.

They both knew the true stakes, and it was not money.

Fargo watched the cards flip out on the table. He wondered when Nance would begin cheating. It took only one quick hand for him to realize Nance had no stomach for a prolonged game and was using marked cards. Fargo placed small bets as he studied the cards and finally figured out the markings.

Nance dealt him a good, pat hand, but Fargo realized it would still be the loser if he left the deck to Nance.

"I'll take three," Fargo said, knowing he would get three kings that Nance had stacked for his own. Nance's eyes widened. He started to complain, then tossed in his hand, letting Fargo win the pot. Nance glared when he realized Fargo had figured out the markings on the deck and was using them to counter his own cheating.

Nance dealt another hand, then pushed forward all of his chips.

"Let's see how much stomach you have for real gambling," Nance said. A murmur of approval went up among the Sydney Ducks watching.

Fargo knew what Nance had in his hand—and it was a lesser hand than the one Fargo held. Something more than a marked deck was in play now.

"I'll call," Fargo said. Then he moved like lightning, his hands catching Nance's wrists and crushing them to the table.

"What's going on?" Nance said. "You—"

"He's got cards stuck to the underside of the table. How many of you have lost to him when he cheated like this?"

"He's lying! I don't have to cheat to beat this whoreson!" shouted Nance, trying to pull free. Fargo let him go so the gambler tumbled back. Fargo grabbed the table edge and pulled up toward him as he stood.

The growl of anger that went around the circle of the Sydney Ducks told Fargo he had been right. Nance had stuck high cards there that everyone could see once Fargo had pointed them out.

"You son of a bitch!" cried Nance. The leader of the Ducks fumbled inside his jacket and drew a small pistol.

Nance was just a fraction of a second too slow. Fargo slapped leather, got out his six-shooter, and fired. Nance grunted at the impact of the bullet, but he wasn't giving up. Hand shaking, he aimed and fired, missing Fargo's head by a hair. Fargo's second shot ended Nance's foul life.

For a moment there was complete silence in the Cobweb Palace. Then pandemonium broke out. The gang tried to rush Fargo. He danced back, let them fall past him off-balance onto the floor and saw others fighting with each other. There seemed no rhyme or reason to the fighting, but Fargo found himself caught up in it, struggling to stay alive.

The Sydney Ducks swung clubs and knives with wild abandon. Only once more did one of the gang draw a six-shooter on Fargo. They shot it out, and the Sydney Duck ended up on the losing end, as had Nance.

Fargo wanted out, but saw no way to cross the saloon and get through the canvas flap to the relative safety of the dock.

The fighting ebbed and flowed and came back in his direction. Slowly, the Sydney Ducks realized he had killed their leader and they ought to exact punishment for his crime. Fargo fought well but was being overwhelmed by sheer numbers when a shrill whistle blast cut through the roar of the melee. A dozen Specials burst into the Cobweb Palace, using their clubs to quell the fighting.

At their head Fargo spotted Hayworth. The Special and four others made their way toward him. Fargo's six-gun was empty, and there had not been time to reload. He faced the Special with balled fists, and knew this was going to be the fight of his life. Probably the last fight.

A Sydney Duck rushed Fargo, only to fall facedown on the floor as Hayworth clubbed him savagely. The Special grinned when he saw Nance's body on the floor.

"You shoot him, Fargo?"

"Yes." Fargo saw no reason to lie.

"The Ducks need a good leader with Nance dead. I'm the man," Hayworth said. Fargo didn't bother replying. There was nothing he could say about his grab for control of the vicious gang. He doubted Hayworth could keep power for long, but that wasn't his problem. Staying alive was.

Then help came from an unlikely source.

Hayworth tapped him on the shoulder with his lead-weighted club and said in a low voice, "Hit the floor. And keep going, if you know what's good for you. Thanks for snuffin' that son of a bitch for me!"

Hayworth landed a heavy blow that numbed Fargo's shoulder. It took no coaxing to sag under the impact. Fargo hit the board floor and saw a small metal ring. He worked his finger through it and tugged open a trapdoor.

"See you in hell, Fargo!" Hayworth called. Then the Special blew another blast on his whistle to summon even more Specials and waded into the center of the fracas.

Fargo slithered through the trapdoor like a snake, found a ladder in the darkness under the Cobweb Palace floor and slammed the door over his head. Heavy footfalls told him he was barely in time. If he had closed the trap door a second later, he would have had unwanted company.

Fargo went down the splintery, rotted ladder and found a small dock. He smiled. He saw a small rowboat tied to the pier. He wasted no time getting into the boat and unshipping the oars. He pushed away from the pier and then began rowing into the fog. The sounds of the fight and the bright light spilling from inside the Cobweb Palace faded as the fog swallowed all sight of the dock and land.

For half an hour Fargo rowed until his back ached and his hands were stiff from gripping the oars. Then he turned toward shore and beached the boat. It took the better part of twenty minutes for him to figure out where he was. To his surprise he had come to ground near the end of Market Street. His stride long and purposeful, he returned to the Regent Hotel as the sun rose to burn away the thick fog.

He went to the clerk and said, "Send my bill to Mr. McGuire at the Montgomery Street Melodeon. He's taking care of Miss Fredericks's bill, also."

"Yes, sir. I've got that noted about her bill, but not yours."

"Mr. McGuire's had a lot on his mind," Fargo said in a confidential tone. For all that he had done, McGuire owed him far more than the price of even this fancy hotel room. He went to the second floor, gathered his gear and left the hotel with no regrets, not even bothering to look in on Amanda and Watkins.

He went down the street to the livery and found his Ovaro waiting patiently for him.

"I never meant to abandon you," he said, giving the pinto a few lumps of sugar he found in his saddlebags. "We're getting out of town pronto."

He saddled the stallion, led it from the stables after leaving a note for the owner that Horatio McGuire was taking care of the livery bill, mounted, and then headed for the theater.

Fargo sat astraddle his horse, feeling more at peace than he had in weeks and wondered if he should keep riding. Then he dismounted, got what he sought from his saddlebags, and went up the familiar steps to the backstage door.

Reggie answered his knock.

"Where you been, Fargo? You look like you've been drug through a knothole backwards."

"I've been taking care of business," Fargo said. "McGuire doesn't have to worry about Nance or the Sydney Ducks anymore."

"How'd that happen? Tell me all 'bout it, man!" demanded Reggie.

Fargo put his finger to his lips to quiet the garrulous old man. For a moment Fargo fancied he could hear Amanda answering a curtain call from the wildly applauding audience for a second bow. He remembered how he had felt onstage during his brief stand-in role.

The momentary flight of fancy passed, and Fargo knew they were alone in the theater.

"I want you to give this to Amanda," Fargo said, handing Reggie the lacquer box he had brought halfway across the country.

Reggie held it at arm's length to study it, looking surprised at Fargo's sudden generosity.

"Why don't you give it to her yourself?"

"She's . . . occupied right now," Fargo said, remembering how Amanda had lain naked alongside Watkins. She might have slept with the young reporter to get a good review, but Fargo didn't think so. Things changed fast in the theater, and he had been lucky to cross paths with Amanda when he had.

"The reporter fella, eh?" Reggie said, peering at Fargo closely. "So he decided to stay on the theater beat? You ain't so broke up over it, are you?"

"I have to go," Fargo said simply.

"You're quite a man, Fargo." Reggie looked at him for a moment, then said, "I'm gonna miss you."

"Good-bye," Fargo said, shaking the old man's hand.

Fargo got to the bottom of the steps, mounted his trusty Ovaro and headed out of San Francisco, traveling south since he didn't want to wait for the ferry to Oakland. This impatience to leave would add a few days to his trip, but Fargo didn't mind.

A day or a week longer to reach the freedom offered by the

Sierra Nevadas did not matter. Putting San Francisco behind him did—with its bad memories . . . and the very, very good ones.

LOOKING FORWARD!
**The following is the opening
section from the next novel in the exciting
Trailsman series from Signet:**

THE TRAILSMAN #241
TEXAS BLOOD MONEY

*Texas, 1859—
Where the pen is mightier than the sword
and the loaded gun is the mightiest of them all.*

Skye Fargo was starting to get annoyed. Finally he turned to
Eddie Buzzell, "You're crazy if you want to go any further.
You might take a hunk of lead right between the eyes."

"I'm paid to take those kinds of chances, Mr. Fargo, just
like you are," Buzzell said, and started scribbling on his
damned notepad again. In the dark.

"Not these kinds of chances, Buzzell. Listen to me,"
Fargo said.

Eddie Buzzell listened. The man was a good listener.

"Those are the Danby boys camping down there in that dry
wash," Fargo continued. "Three of the meanest bushwhacking
kill-crazy devils to draw breath in the state of Texas. Those
boys've slaughtered, robbed, raped, and burned their way
down from Nebraska. They—"

Damn it all, Buzzell was scribbling in his notebook again.
That's all he ever did.

Buzzell said, writing furiously, "Robbed, raped, and burned
their way across the frontier. Beautiful. Then what?"

Fargo angrily snatched the notepad from Buzzell's hands and flung it into the bushes. Buzzell opened his mouth to protest, and Fargo clamped his and over it, grabbing Buzzell in a very uncomfortable headlock.

"Listen to me, you ignorant New York pimplehead," he whispered into Buzzell's left ear. "The Danbys would just as soon blast your head off than spit on a bug. They're mean, Eddie, very mean. Ain't nobody been able to take 'em, not the rangers, not the cavalry, not any of the twelve bounty boys they planted six feet under. But that's okay Eddie, because I'm gonna take 'em myself. There's two thousand dollars apiece on their heads, dead or alive. That's six thousand dollars, my friend, just enough for a long and relaxing vacation anywhere I want. You ain't even carrying a piece, not that you'd know how to use it if you did. Be a good boy and stay right here till the shooting stops. I don't come back a minute later, I ain't at all. You hightail it back to town and get your skinny ass on a train back East. Them's the rules."

He released Buzzell, who went scrambling through the bushes to find his notepad.

"Make a little more noise, why don't you?" Fargo said.

Buzzell found his notepad and started writing in it again. "I won't get in your way, Mr. Fargo," he said. "You won't even know I'm there."

Fargo was satisfied that his firepower was ready. "It's your ass, Eddie, and I ain't responsible for it. You follow me in, you're doin' it at your own risk. Whatever happens, just remember I tried talkin' you out of it."

"I appreciate that, Mr. Fargo," Buzzell said, "I really do. But I have my job to do and you have yours. I can take care of myself."

"All right," Fargo said. "It's your funeral. Just—"

Shots rang out from what sounded like several directions, one of them whizzing so close that Fargo could smell the gun smoke.

Excerpt from *Texas Blood Money*

"Stay down," Fargo shouted at Buzzell, diving for cover into the bushes. Damn wet-behind-the-ears city punk had blown Fargo's cover. Fargo pumped the Remington twice in the direction of the belching gunfire down in the wash, and heard an audible grunt.

He slid through the thick underbrush like a greased snake in the direction of the silenced gunshots, clutching the shotgun in one fist. He circled the Danbys' cookfire from eighty yards off, the fire deserted now, bedrolls empty. Shots were ringing out from behind him and off to the west now. The Danbys were firing blind, not hard to do on a dark night with no moonlight. Fargo had waited for just a night like this, knowing the Danbys weren't going anywhere. Isaac had been spotted in a town called Swayzee three days ago, no doubt checking out the spoils.

A month ago, Eddie Buzzell showed up in town and began following Fargo around, asking questions and writing stuff down on that stupid little notepad. A journalist from New York City he was, and wanted to write about Fargo's many adventures for the magazines back East.

When Fargo got wind that the dreaded Danbys were sleazing around in his backyard and had a sizable bounty on them, he volunteered his services. Six thousand dollars was six thousand dollars, not to mention ridding the territory of the scurviest bunch of murderers since the Clantons.

And now here he was, pinned down by their gunfire. This wasn't going well at all, and he had Eddie Buzzell to blame.

He made his way over to a clump of live oak, leaned up against it, and began to reload the Remington. He knew he had to go to Plan B—trouble was, he had no Plan B.

He crawled silently toward a patch where the undergrowth was the thickest. Halfway there, he came upon the lifeless body of Willis Danby, a huge chunk of his neck missing, the last of his blood spurting into the dirt. His mouth was open, and Lord did he have a lot of rotten teeth.

It was one lucky shot, all things considered.

"Willis!" he heard one of the other Danbys bellow. He looked up and saw Isaac Danby, all six and a half feet of him, charging down the wash, wielding a huge hachet—taking Fargo's head off was his only goal in life.

"You killed him, you son of a whore!" Isaac bellowed, and was on Fargo like beans on rice. He dived at Fargo, swinging the hatchet. Fargo ducked and rolled to the left, and Isaac Danby landed on dirt.

There was no time to use the Remington, so Fargo let it fall from his fist. He jerked the pistol out of his holster but not soon enough. Isaac pounced on him and curled his fingers around Fargo's gullet, squeezing with everything he had, filthy long fingernails digging into the soft flesh.

Fargo ripped at Isaac's greasy black hair and came away with a chunk. Isaac could have cared less. He kept squeezing Fargo's neck, successfully cutting off his wind.

Fargo rammed his thumb into Isaac's left eye, digging in deep until he felt flesh rupture. Isaac wailed in agony, taking his hands from Fargo's neck and covering his face.

Fargo thrust up with his fist and slammed Isaac Danby in the throat. Isaac tumbled away, a gurgled sound escaped him as he fell, the likes of which Fargo would never forget. It was as if somebody slapped a slab of beef liver against a flat rock.

Fargo drew his pistol, trying to clear his head, and Isaac pounced on him anew. Fargo managed to squeeze off one shot, which stopped Isaac in midstep, taking him squarely in the gut. Isaac dropped like a block of ice, but not for long. Even a solid gut-shot from five feet away couldn't keep a Danby down.

Isaac rose to his knees and went for his Colt. A dark patch of blood covered half his face.

Fargo wasted no time in putting a second bullet into Isaac Danby, this time right through his good eye, completely robbing him of his sight, along with half his face.

Blinded and beaten, Isaac stood motionless. The Colt slipped from his fingers, but he did manage to stay alive long enough to pull out a shiny new pigsticker tucked into his belt with his other hand. He raised the knife a foot or so, then pitched forward into the dirt, raising a puff of brown dust, as dead as dead can be. The knife skittered across the ground a couple of feet from Fargo's foot.

"I'm getting too old for this," Fargo muttered. He sat up, rubbing his sore neck, and replaced the two bullets he'd put into Isaac Danby.

He gave the barrel a spin, ready for action.

A shot barked behind him. Fargo saw the white blast of a pistol out of the corner of his eye. Pain exploded in his right shoulder. He went sprawling face first onto the ground. The Colt flew from his hand.

"Shit," Fargo growled, already in agony. A pair of dusty boots appeared before him.

"I got to say, I am very impressed."

There was no anger in the words, no malice. Fargo made himself look up, and found himself staring into the face of Earl Danby, one of the youngers of the Danby tribe. Just my luck, Fargo thought, feeling his life's juices squirting from his wounded shoulder.

"Who are you?" Earl Danby asked, tucking the twin barrels of his shotgun under Fargo's chin and raising his head up another few inches.

Fargo looked up at the younger Danby. He was smaller than his brothers, ferret-faced and scrawny, though Fargo had no doubts he was just as mean.

"I wanna look the man who killed my brothers right in the eyes," Earl Danby said, cocking his pistol and aiming it straight at Fargo's head. "Just so's the last thing he sees before he burns in hell is one of the Danby boys."

He aimed the twin barrels of his rifle in the middle of Fargo's forehead. Fargo squeezed his eyes shut. He'd failed, as he'd never failed before, and this particular failure meant certain death.

What a stupid way to die, Fargo thought just as he heard the dry click of Earl Danby's shotgun. Fargo's eyes opened wide. He still had a chance.

"Shit," Earl Danby said. He tossed his shotgun aside and went for his pistol. Fargo took the opportunity to roll to the left and go for Isaac's knife.

Earl fired off a shot that kicked up dust an inch from Fargo's nose. Fargo snatched the knife, rolled onto his back, and flung it skillfully. He took the outlaw squarely in the balls.

Earl Danby let out a wail laced with pain, and yanked out the knife. Blood spurted from between his legs. He dropped the pistol and grabbed his wounded sweetmeats.

"Damn that must hurt," Fargo commented, scrambling for Earl's gun. Earl sank to his knees, wailing like a stuck pig and started whimpering like a little baby, trying unsuccessfully to staunch the flow of blood from his crotch.

Fargo wasted not a second, snatching up the gun and scrambling to his feet. He aimed it directly at Earl Danby's head. Earl hardly seemed to notice, or even care, concentrating not on impending death but rather the incredible pain from between his legs.

Earl Danby ceased to be, for the time being, an immediate threat to Fargo's health. Fat tears were rolling down his dirty face now, leaving clean streaks that Fargo could see even in the moonlight.

"Stop crying, Earl," Fargo said with a little heat. "It ain't becomin' to an outlaw of your stature."

"You shot my pecker all to hell, you stinkin' bastard," Earl Danby wailed, blood seeping through his fingers.

Fargo kept the gun trained on Danby's head. He wouldn't kill the last Danby brother unless he got stupid, a distinct possibility.

"I didn't shoot it, Earl," Fargo said. "Doubt I could find it if I tried."

"How'm I a-gonna get any women now?" Earl cried, clutching himself.

Excerpt from *Texas Blood Money*

It was exactly the kind of question Fargo had expected from the likes of a Danby. He said, "Earl, havin' sex is about to become the very least of your problems."

He kicked Earl square on the chin, the tip of his boot connecting solidly with Earl's lower jaw. Still on his knees, Earl flopped face first into the dirt, sickeningly dazed but still conscious. Fargo hog-tied the bastard, rendering him trouble free.

Earl spit out some dirt and said, "Stranger, the day's a-gonna come when I get me the chance to do to you what you done to me. Only thing is, I'm a-gonna cut your pecker off an' feed it to a dawg."

Fargo kicked Earl Danby hard in the ribs. Earl cried out in agony. Fargo grabbed him by the hair and yanked him forward, Earl screaming every inch of the way.

Fargo jabbed the barrel of the pistol into Earl's left ear. Earl whimpered.

"You make me feel tired all over, Earl," Fargo said. "I don't want any more of it. Behave yourself and maybe you'll live long enough to hang."

Fargo whacked Earl Danby on the side of his head with the business end of the pistol and left him facedown in the dirt.

"I had a friend with me, Earl," Fargo said, ready to adorn west Texas with the contents of Earl Danby's skull. "A fella from back East, name of Buzzell. You seen him?"

Earl Danby barely managed to shake his head, he was too busy blubbering like a babe. Fargo was just about disgusted. There was a time when an outlaw worth his salt would accept his fate and still act like a man. Earl Danby was a disgrace to the memory of a lot of fast but dead hardcases that littered every Boot Hill in the West.

Fargo went looking and moments later found Eddie Buzzell flat on his back, deader than dead could be. A slug had taken out a nice chunk of his neck, and he'd bled to death in minutes. His eyes were open in an expression of disbelief. The notebook was still clenched in his left fist.

Fargo plucked the notebook from Buzzell and found the

pencil in the dirt a foot or so away. Fargo started scribbling in the notebook, then tucked it into his vest pocket. "I'm sorry, city boy. I tried to warn you. But you still died in the saddle," Fargo said. He looked at the lifeless body with some affection and added, "You were a credit to your profession, Eddie."

Fargo went back to where Earl Danby was drooling into the dirt and pulled the Arkansas toothpick from his boot. He let Earl follow the razor-sharp blade with fearful eyes, teasing him enough with each movement to squeeze out some extra tears. Fargo pulled his arm back and, in one fluid motion, swung forward. The trusted knife slashed the air.

Fargo pulled tight on the rope shackling Earl's hands. "Get up, Earl," he said. "It's late and I'm tired."

Earl Danby grudgingly got to his feet. Fargo kicked him in the general direction of Hambone. Earl started walking, and Fargo followed.

"You really think I'm a-gonna hang?" Earl wanted to know.

Feeling truly tired, Fargo said, "If the good people of Mineral Springs have anything to say about it, most likely."

Fargo gave Earl Danby another series of swift kicks in the butt until Earl started moving a little faster.

SIGNET BOOKS

JUDSON GRAY

Introducing a brand-new post-Civil War western
saga from the author of the Hunter Trilogy...

DOWN TO MARROWBONE

Jim McCutcheon had squandered his Southern family's fortune
and had to find a way to rebuild it among the boomtowns.
Jake Penn had escaped the bonds of slavery and had to find
his long-lost sister...
Together, they're an unlikely team—but with danger down
every trail, nothing's worth more than a friend you can count
on...

❑ 0-451-20158-2/$5.99